"Somet... worrying you, Luke."

Fleur couldn't help wondering about the frown on his face and his silence. "You've scarcely spoken since we left Rivermoon."

"Boorish, am I?" he asked.

"I didn't say that, but you do appear to have something on your mind."

"Would it surprise you to know that you're part of it?"

"Not at all, your frown hints that your thoughts are unpleasant—and I can still sense your underlying antagonism toward me," Fleur added bleakly, turning to stare unseeingly at trees lining the riverbank. Somehow the joy of being taken out was slipping away.

"Antagonism? I've never felt actual antagonism toward you," he said soberly. "Haven't there been moments when you've sensed that my feelings have been—just the opposite?"

Dear Reader:

We hope our December Harlequin Romances bring you many hours of enjoyment this holiday season.

1989 was an exciting year. We published our 3000th Harlequin Romance! And we introduced a new cover design—which we hope you like.

We're wrapping up the year with a terrific selection of satisfying stories, written by your favorite authors, as well as by some very talented newcomers we're introducing to the series. As always, we've got settings guaranteed to take you places—from the English Cotswolds, to New Zealand, to Holland, to some hometown settings in the United States.

So when you need a break from the hustle and bustle of preparing for the holidays, sit back and relax with our heartwarming stories. Stories with laughter...a few tears...and lots of heart.

And later, when you get a chance, drop us a line with your thoughts and ideas about how we can try to make your enjoyment of Harlequin Romances even better in the years to come.

From our house to yours, Happy Holidays! And may this special season bring you a lasting gift of joy and happiness.

The Editors
Harlequin Romance
225 Duncan Mill Road
Don Mills, Ontario, Canada
M3B 3K9

RIDDELL
OF RIVERMOON

Miriam MacGregor

Harlequin Books

TORONTO • NEW YORK • LONDON
AMSTERDAM • PARIS • SYDNEY • HAMBURG
STOCKHOLM • ATHENS • TOKYO • MILAN

Original hardcover edition published in 1989
by Mills & Boon Limited

ISBN 0-373-03022-3

Harlequin Romance first edition December 1989

CHAPTER ONE

THE dominating air of the tall man who strode into the florist's shop was not lost upon Fleur, and as he approached the counter she was struck by the clean-cut appearance of his handsome face. He was dark-haired, and his black brows formed bars above dark grey eyes. As Fleur looked up at his straight nose and sensuous mouth she was reminded of the classical features depicted on Roman or Greek deities.

Yet there was something vaguely familiar about him, something she was unable to define, and this fact puzzled her because she felt sure she had never met him before these moments. If she *had* met him previously, she also knew that here was a man she would not have forgotten.

He stood regarding her in silence while scrutinising her straight dark brown hair which she wore bobbed with a fringe, and the line of her dark brows arching above large blue eyes shadowed by thick black lashes. Her clear complexion and slightly retroussé nose came in for his consideration, and when his eyes lingered upon the curve of her generous but sweet mouth, a flush rose to her cheeks.

'Can I help you?' she asked, feeling compelled to bring his examination to an end.

'I doubt it.' The voice was deep, the tone abrupt.

'Oh.' She was nonplussed, wondering why he had come into the shop. His next words enlightened her.

'I wish to see Mrs Fleming. Is she here?'

'No, I'm afraid she's out at the moment, but she'll be back soon.'

'I'll wait.' The reply held a touch of impatience as he

picked up a catalogue of New Zealand native trees and shrubs.

Watching him browse through its pages she saw him pause to look at illustrations of the yellow kowhai tree and the brilliant scarlet manuka shrub, and while she returned to her task of arranging a bouquet to go to a hospital patient she continued to observe him from beneath her lashes.

He was not in the habit of being kept waiting, especially by a woman, she decided. Or did some other matter niggle at him? She sensed a subdued restlessness in his examination of the potted cyclamen and chrysanthemums, and the drooping plants suspended by chains from the ceiling.

And then, having replaced the catalogue on the counter, he moved to stand before the display of gift baskets that rested upon shelves running the length of the shop. They were in different shapes and sizes, some being softly shaded in the various blues, pinks, mauves and yellows of everlasting statice, while others glowed in the reds, golds and bronze of straw flowers.

'She's developed an expert's hand at doing these arrangements,' he remarked over his shoulder.

'She——? I presume you mean my mother. Are you an authority on gift baskets?'

'I've seen a few.'

She said nothing further, deciding there was no need to tell him that she herself had made each one of those baskets, and that they were her special department in the business. Mother had started her on them by encouraging her to play with flowers when she had been a child. Those were the days when Aunt Jessica had been with them. A small sigh of regret escaped her. It was a pity about Aunt Jessica and Mother. It must be ten years since they had spoken to each other.

She brushed Aunt Jessica from her thoughts by spreading

a fresh sheet of green waxed paper to protect a second bouquet ordered for a patient in the hospital. And while she tried to concentrate upon choosing suitable blooms from a nearby plastic bucket of water her thoughts returned to the tall man whose attention was still centred upon the gift baskets.

Why did he wish to see Mother? she wondered. Was he a new company rep who had come seeking orders for floral requirements such as coloured wax papers, fine wiring or ribbons? She doubted it, because the reps usually wore business suits and carried order books, whereas this man wore casual sportswear of dark brown trousers and a check jacket that fitted across his broad shoulders. She also noticed his tanned complexion which suggested an outdoor life. No, definitely not a company rep, she decided.

And then her musings were interrupted when a woman who owned a complex of motels entered the shop. Tall, brisk and businesslike, she went to the gift-basket shelves, selected the largest creation of tawny shades and carried it to the counter.

Fleur smiled at her. 'Good morning, Mrs Gordon. Is this for one of the motels?'

'Yes. I can't keep up with fresh flowers in my entire establishment,' she said in a ringing voice. 'I've decided to put dried arrangements in each of the motels. They're so much less work and will last through the winter when flowers are scarce and expensive.'

'Yes, they certainly become more costly,' Fleur agreed.

'I want your mother to make a survey of the rooms. I'd like her to decide upon which sizes and colours should go where.'

'Very well. I'm sure Mother will be pleased to confer with you.' Again Fleur saw no necessity to point out that this was her own department, because people like to think their needs were being attended to by the boss. It made them feel important.

'Your mother is out at the moment, Fleur?'

'Yes, she's collecting colour details for the Meredith wedding. It'll fill the motels for miles around.'

'I'm already booked for it. Please ask your mother if she can come before midday tomorrow.'

'I'll do that.' She wrote a few details in a notebook.

Mrs Gordon left the shop carrying the gift basket which had been protected from the April winds by yellow waxed paper, and Fleur continued with the task of finishing the hospital bouquet. Moments later a nearby movement caught her eye, and she looked up to discover that the man waiting to see her mother had returned to the counter.

He regarded her steadily before he said, 'So you're Fleur—Fleur, short for Fleurette.'

The remark was so unexpected she was taken by surprise. 'Yes——'

'You were named after this florist's shop, the Fleurette.'

She sighed, sending a rueful glance towards the gold lettering on the shop window, and she then noticed that his mouth had tightened while his eyes looked at her with cold disapproval. Feeling disconcerted, she said defensively, 'I'm afraid I had no say in the name my mother chose to bestow upon me at birth.' And then she wondered why she tried to excuse the name that she herself had never really liked, because it had caused part of the trouble between her mother and aunt.

The man said nothing, although he continued to regard her with eyes that had become cynical, and he then turned away from the counter as though having no wish for further conversation with her.

His attitude came as a surprise to Fleur. She was not unused to being observed by males, and while she never considered herself to be beautiful she knew she possessed a little something that attracted them. But this man appeared to be holding resentment against her for some reason and the fact puzzled her.

However, she decided to ignore it, and clutching at her dignity she drew herself up to her full five feet two inches as she glanced at her watch and said, 'I'm sorry Mother is taking so long to return. Are you sure I'm unable to help you? I mean—if it's a matter of sending a single red rosebud to a lady each day——'

A snort of derision escaped him. 'That's most unlikely.'

'Perhaps you're looking for a gift? Some of the pot plants bloom well into the winter, or a maidenhair fern is always popular.'

'Nor am I here to purchase a gift.' His words had become clipped with irritation. 'I told you, I'm here to see Mrs Fleming. Joyce, isn't it?'

'Yes, Mother's name is Joyce.' She looked at him wonderingly.

He sent her a cool glance. 'The fact that I'm not making a purchase irks you?'

'Certainly not. I was merely trying to help,' she returned quietly, her chin held slightly higher.

'I'm afraid it's out of your hands to do so. It's a job for your mother. I need her assistance—*if* she'll give it.'

'I can assure you that Mother is always ready to give assistance,' Fleur declared with confidence.

'She might not be so ready this time.' His tone had become abrupt.

Fleur watched him in silence, waiting to be given more information, but as it was not forthcoming she sent another glance towards her watch as she said, 'It's almost lunch time. I'm sure she'll be here at any moment.'

The words had hardly left her lips when she saw her mother's car draw into the kerbside. She watched as Joyce locked the vehicle before coming into the shop, then felt a surge of surprise to see her mother stand still while she stared at the man. It was almost, Fleur thought, as though she knew him.

Fleur spoke quickly. 'This gentleman has been waiting to see you, Mother. He appears to need your help in some way.'

But it seemed as if Joyce had hardly heard the remark. Slim and dark-haired, she was an older version of Fleur, and as her blue eyes surveyed the man she asked, 'Have we met? Or is it just that you're the image of somebody I know?'

His face remained impassive. 'I'm like somebody you know—my late father's twin brother, Robert Riddell.'

'*Uncle Bob*——' Fleur exclaimed. 'Why didn't you tell me?'

He sent her a cool glance. 'Because my business is not with you. It's with your mother.' He turned to Joyce. 'I'm Luke Riddell.'

Joyce made no effort to hide her interest. 'You've come from Wanganui? How is Bob? You could be taken for his son.'

'Since Dad died he's been like a father to me.' He paused, waiting for her to say something further before he added, 'I notice you don't ask after my uncle's wife—your sister.'

Joyce stiffened. 'Jessica? I doubt that she'll have changed very much. People don't, do they?'

Watching him, Fleur became aware of a sudden conviction which made her ask, 'Are you seeking help for Aunt Jessica?'

'Well, you could say it concerns her.'

'She's all right?' Joyce asked quickly. 'She's not ill?'

'She's not really ill,' he assured her, 'although I can't say she's all right. The point is, she needs your help.'

'Then why doesn't she phone and ask for it?' Joyce demanded drily.

'I did suggest it to her.'

'But stubbornness won the day,' Joyce cut in with a touch

of irony. 'Are you aware that we haven't spoken to each other for ten years?'

Luke regarded her steadily. 'Isn't life too short for sisters to behave in that fashion?'

Joyce's manner became cold. 'I'll have you know I've written to her *three times*, but not one reply have I had in return.'

'You didn't think of paying her a visit? After all, Wanganui is not a great distance from this city of Palmerston North. In fact we're little more than fifty miles away.'

'Would I have been welcome? I doubt it,' Joyce retorted.

He was silent, frowning at her until he said, 'Perhaps she considers you owe her more than letters or a visit.'

'What would give you that impression?' Joyce asked mildly.

He shrugged. 'Oh, just the numerous hints that have been dropped here and there.'

Joyce stared at him incredulously. 'Hints implying that I owe Jessica?'

'I suppose you could put it like that.' He watched her narrowly.

'Hasn't Bob explained the situation between Jessica and me?'

'Bless him, his main aim is to avoid trouble.'

'And that means keeping his mouth shut if my name happens to crop up,' Joyce said with understanding. 'Dear old Bob, he always tried to keep the peace.' She smiled as reminiscences appeared to flit through her mind, then her tone became brisk as she said, 'You'd better have lunch with us. Fleur will put mugs of soup in the microwave oven and we'll have heated ham, cheese and tomato-filled croissants followed by coffee.'

'Thank you, that's very kind,' he murmured.

'It's no trouble,' Joyce assured him. 'Besides, I want to

hear more about Jessica. You said she needs help. You can tell me about it while we're having lunch.' She almost dismissed him by turning her attention to the notebook on the counter. 'Ah, I see that more flowers have been ordered for hospital patients, Fleur. I'll attend to them while you fix the lunch.'

Fleur turned to Luke Riddell. 'Would you like to come out to our workroom?' she asked with studied politeness, then added in explanation, 'I do flower arrangements at the counter only when I'm alone in the shop, otherwise I can't see when anyone comes in.'

He followed her into the back room, then looked about him with interest. At one end a stainless-steel bench and sink had high stools pushed beneath it, while a microwave oven rested between a fridge and a cupboard containing dishes.

'We always have lunch here,' she said while washing her hands at the sink, then, when he did not reply, she turned to find him gazing up at the galaxy of colour hanging in bunches from the ceiling.

'It's like an inverted garden,' he remarked at last.

She smiled. 'Those are the everlasting flowers for the gift baskets and dried arrangements. We tie them in bunches according to their colour and species, then suspend them from hooks in wire netting attached to the ceiling.' She named the various species then finished by saying, 'That fuzzy white is gypsophila, or baby's breath, and those lovely bright orange things are what we call Chinese lanterns.'

'I am familiar with the species. Bob grows them for Jess. You climb a ladder to get each bunch?'

'No. We have a pole with a hook that lifts them down, although it's easier to use the ladder when putting them back.' She paused then indicated a doorway. 'If you'd like to wash your hands there's a handbasin and toilet through there.'

'Thank you.' He disappeared into their washroom.

She began to prepare the lunch, but found her mind refusing to veer from the handsome face of the tall visitor. He's a man who can be demanding when it suits him, or pleasant when the occasion calls for it, she mused. As for that sensuous mouth—no doubt there's a woman in Wanganui who is well aware of that mouth.

She pushed the thought away, her eyes narrowing as she tried to recall the reason for Aunt Jessica's departure to Wanganui. Hadn't somebody died, causing Uncle Bob to move there? Somebody connected with Luke Riddell, she now realised.

His return cut into her thoughts and she knew that he continued to examine the room, his eyes wandering towards a shelf of different-gauged fine wiring, and to a long wall-rod which held rolls of satin-like ribbons in a variety of colours. There were numerous gift baskets waiting to be filled, and there was a carton of ceramic plant-holders ready to be placed on display in the shop.

His survey caused her to say, 'I'm afraid it's all somewhat cluttered through lack of space.'

His face remained unsmiling. 'Nevertheless your mother appears to have quite a cosy business. It's no wonder that Jess felt she'd been—done in the eye.'

For a moment she wondered if she had heard correctly, then, as the words registered, her jaw sagged slightly as she turned from the fridge to stare at him in an uncomprehending manner. '*Done in the eye*? I'm afraid I don't understand.'

His manner became cool. 'Or is it that you have no wish to understand?' Then before she could find words he went on, 'Fortunately Jessica's windfall in one of the Golden Kiwi lotteries gave her a lift. It helped to compensate for everything she'd lost.'

Fleur betrayed surprise. 'Oh? She had a win? That must have been exciting for her.'

'You didn't know?'

'No. Didn't Mother tell you that Aunt hasn't communicated with us at all since she went to live in Wanganui? I hope it was a good prize, something really worth winning.'

He grinned. 'A cool two hundred thousand dollars, thank you very much. It made her feel that life wasn't a series of hard knocks after all. Naturally, it's been well invested.'

'Are you saying she has suffered hard knocks since living in Wanganui?'

'No. I mean that things were tough for her before she left Palmerston North and moved to Wanganui. But you probably know about her troubles during those days.'

Fleur's eyes widened as she stared at him. 'What you are *really* saying is that she suffered hard blows when she was in business with Mother?'

'Well, didn't she?'

'I can't remember any blows being suffered by Aunt Jess,' she declared with a hint of indignation in her voice.

'Perhaps you prefer to—forget? Or don't you consider that losing her right to the business she'd built up could be called a hard blow?

She shook her head in bewilderment. 'I don't know what you're talking about, Mr Riddell, but believe me, you've got your wires crossed somewhere. Something tells me you've been fed incorrect information.'

He looked at her with amused tolerance. 'Are you sure your own knowledge of the situation is correct?'

'I have a fair idea of what happened, even if it is ten years since Aunt was here and I was only twelve when she left.'

'Which makes you twenty-two years of age now,' he commented. 'I'm ten years older than you.' He paused, then added reminiscently, 'When I was your age my father died. It was one of the reasons for Bob's move from Palmerston North to Wanganui.' He fell silent, his grey eyes seeming to look into the past until he said, 'With Dad's death I inherited Rivermoon, but at twenty-two I was inexperienced, so Bob came to advise me in the running of the place.'

'Rivermoon is an unusual name.' Somehow it caught her

fancy.

'It's a farm property on the River Road which runs along the eastern bank of the Wanganui River. It's shaped like a crescent moon. The front flat land follows a bend in the river, then rises to hills at the back.'

'Your father had become ill?' The question was forced from her by her naturally sympathetic nature.

He shook his head gloomily. 'I doubt that he'd ever had a day's illness in his life. It was a riding accident. My mother was unable to cope with her grief. She became ill and died the following year.'

'Losing both parents so quickly must have been ghastly for you,' Fleur said in a low voice.

'I don't know how I got on to this subject,' he admitted gruffly. 'It's a topic I usually avoid.'

'You were saying that your father's death was only one of the reasons that took Uncle Bob to Wanganui,' Fleur reminded him.

'Well, naturally, the other reason was Jessica. He felt he had to get her away from Palmerston North where she was so unhappy.'

Fleur frowned as she took the soup out of the microwave oven. 'I remember that she always seemed to be cross about something.'

'And you didn't know why?' His tone had become mocking.

'Well, there was her dissatisfaction over the business situation.'

'Ah, yes, the Fleurette appears to have been the crux of the matter. Can you remember those days?'

She was indignant. 'Of course I can remember them.'

'But are you sure you were told all the details concerning the trouble? At the time you were little more than a child, and adults don't usually confide such matters to children.'

The truth of his words startled her. Yes, she *had* been a mere child at the time, therefore it seemed unlikely that Mother would confide in her to the fullest extent. Yet she felt sure she understood why her aunt had always been in a bad mood, therefore she said, 'If you *must* know, Aunt Jessica's discontent stemmed from Mother's ownership of this business.'

'I'll bet it did, and that's just the point. I understand that the business had been Jessica's baby, built up by her own energy.' His words held the ring of an accusation.

A gasp of indignation escaped her. 'That's utter rubbish. Mother pulled her weight.'

'So how did Jessica lose the business to her sister?' His eyes became cold as he awaited her answer.

Fleur glared at him. 'I have no intention of discussing this private matter with you, but if you're really keen to learn details you should go to Uncle Bob. I'm sure he can give you the full story.'

'I'm afraid he refuses to discuss the subject. He says it's all in the past and he doesn't want any unpleasantness dragged up. He was even against my plan of asking your mother for help.'

'You're saying it wasn't Aunt Jessica who sent you?'

'No. She scoffed at the idea, declaring your mother would never raise a finger to help her.' He broke off as Joyce entered the workroom.

If she heard his words she ignored them by speaking to Fleur. 'I've completed the remaining flower orders for the hospital, dear. You can deliver them after lunch. Is the soup ready?'

'Yes, and the croissants have been heated.'

Joyce pulled the stools from beneath the bench and took paper napkins from a drawer. She then smiled at Luke and said, 'Please sit down and tell me about this help that has suddenly become so very necessary after ten years of silence.'

He looked at Joyce with a hint of disapproval. 'If you haven't communicated with your sister you'll not know that she has developed arthritis.'

'Really? That's unfortunate for her.'

'Indeed it is, especially as it is in her hands. Her fingers won't work as they used to. They've become painful, causing her to fumble and work slowly, and now she's behind with her orders.'

'Orders? I'm afraid I still haven't got the complete picture,' Joyce pointed out patiently.

'Orders for gift baskets,' he explained. 'As soon as she became settled at Rivermoon she made several which she took to the florist's shops in Wanganui. Apparently they sold well and she's been kept busy ever since. Bob grows the flowers she needs.' He gazed up at the colourful masses hanging from the ceiling. 'We have most of these flowers hanging in a shed. Air-drying, she calls it. However, she has suddenly found herself with a deadline to meet, something like a dozen baskets to be ready by Thursday afternoon.'

Joyce, ever practical, said briskly, 'Why doesn't she employ someone to help her with the orders, at least until she's climbed over this particular hurdle?'

Fleur added, 'You said she'd had a big lottery win, therefore she could afford to pay someone.' She turned to her mother eagerly. 'Luke says——' She paused as the slipping of his name caused a faint flush to rise to her cheeks, then went on bravely, 'Luke says that Aunt Jessica won two hundred thousand dollars in one of the Golden Kiwi lotteries.'

Joyce was genuinely pleased. 'How lovely for her. She must have been delighted.'

'Yes, we were all happy for her, especially dear old Bob. And she could certainly afford to pay someone, if only she could find a person who could do the work to her satisfaction. I might add that she has tried several people, but their work doesn't suit her.'

Joyce spoke in a dry tone. 'I think I'm beginning to see daylight. The reason for your visit is beginning to seep through. You want *me* to go to Jessica. You're asking *me* to complete the orders that have been requested for Thursday afternoon.'

'Hit fair and square on the nail,' he admitted with a grin.

Fleur spoke quietly. 'I think it's a good idea, Mother. It would help heal the breach between you.'

Luke added persuasively, 'It's a little more than an hour's drive to Rivermoon, and of course you'd be welcome to stay there.' He paused, staring down at his hands before he looked at her earnestly and said, 'There's something else. I feel sure there's more than the baskets troubling her. She appears to be fretting over an inner distress of some sort and I can't help wondering if it's because of the long-standing rift between you.'

Joyce sent him a smile that was full of sweetness. 'If it is she knows what to do, or has her arthritis paralysed her to the extent of being unable to dial our phone number?'

His mouth tightened as he drawled, 'You're quite a tough woman, Joyce Fleming. You don't give an inch. One might almost say you're hard.'

Fleur's blue eyes sparked with sudden anger as she rose to her mother's defence. Her soup mug hit the bench with a slight bang as she snapped at Luke Riddell. 'Don't you *dare* speak to my mother in that manner. It's obvious you don't know anything about the—the business situation, otherwise you wouldn't have had the—the utter cheek to have come here with these suggestions. Let me tell you that the rift between Aunt and Mother was entirely Aunt's fault.'

The cold grey eyes he turned upon her looked like pebbles. 'Are you quite sure?'

'Of course I'm sure.'

'You appear to be as tough as your mother.'

Fleur's voice rose in a fury. 'My mother is not tough, and you have a colossal nerve to say so. Oh, yes, it would satisfy Aunt Jess mightily to see Mother go running to *her*. My oath, how she'd gloat!'

'Be quiet, Fleur,' Joyce snapped sharply.

'That's not easy, Mother. Why don't you tell him about those days?'

'Because they're no longer important to me,' Joyce retorted.

'But it would help him to understand.'

'I'm not in the habit of discussing my private affairs with strangers.'

Fleur kept a grip on her patience. 'He's not really a stranger. He's almost a distant relative because he's Uncle Bob's nephew. They are living with him. His father was Uncle Bob's twin brother. Can't you see that he should be told the true situation?'

'I'm sure Bob will tell him all he needs to know.'

'He says Uncle Bob won't tell him anything,' Fleur reminded Joyce.

'That's because Bob's a dear soul who is loyal to Jessica.'

'Mother, you frustrate me.'

'Well, that's a change. It's usually daughters who frustrate their mothers.'

Luke's voice cut into their conversation. 'I am still here, you know, even if you two appear to have forgotten that small fact.'

Joyce turned to him apologetically. 'I'm sorry, I'm afraid we're being rather rude, but you must understand that your visit has dug into old wounds.'

Fleur looked at Joyce with questions in her eyes. Why didn't she explain the situation to this man? Didn't she realise he considered the quarrel between herself and her sister to be all *her* fault? For some reason she was unable to define, it infuriated Fleur to know he believed her mother to be in the wrong, especially when a few words would clear up the matter.

But would he believe what he was told? Could he be made to understand that it was Aunt Jessica who had been so difficult with her domineering attitudes, and that it was Mother who had been the injured party, at least until the blow-up.

Fleur had always been positive her mother had been in the right, but now she began to wonder if there were facts of which she herself had been unaware. As he had pointed out, she had been a child at the time, so was it just blind loyalty to her mother that made her so sure her parent had been one hundred per cent in the right?

She frowned, trying to think back over the years, and through the haze of her memories she heard Luke express appreciation for their hospitality. Then, as he stood up, she knew he was preparing to leave, but instead of saying goodbye he turned and spoke to her.

'If you intend delivering flowers to the hospital perhaps you'd allow me to drive you there.'

She declined quickly. 'No, thank you. I have my own transport.'

But she had reckoned without her mother, who said, 'Nonsense, Fleur, of course you can be gracious enough to accept such a kind offer—especially after our lack of enthusiasm regarding Luke's request.'

His grey eyes turned to Joyce. 'Then you refuse to give it even the slightest consideration?'

She became exasperated. 'You don't seem to realise you're asking me to neglect my own business to go to Jessica's assitance. What about my own commitments? In the near future I have to do the flowers for a large wedding.'

'You could make arrangements for extra help.'

'If I can find extra help, so can Jessica,' Joyce snapped at him. 'Really, the idea that I should drop everything and go to Wanganui is quite ridiculous.'

'Well, at least I've tried,' he said with a resigned air, then moved to where the three arrangements of cellophane-protected flowers rested on the counter.

Fleur made no further protest as the bouquets were transferred to a blue Volvo which had been left in a nearby parking area. And she told herself it was kind of him to offer to drive her to deliver them at the hospital, especially after his visit had proved to be such a failure. But surely he could understand that an important assignment such as the flowers for a wedding could not be jeopardised for Aunt Jessica's order for gift baskets. Or was he too one-eyed on Aunt's behalf to appreciate this fact?

Strangely, when she was sitting beside him in the car the answers to these questions lost their importance and she became conscious only of the man's presence and the fact that she was near him. From the corner of her eye she could see his hands resting upon the wheel, the long tanned fingers giving an impression of strength.

A slight turn of her head showed his profile, and again she admired its classical lines. Pull yourself together, she snapped at herself in a silent reprimand. You're like a twittery schoolgirl. Try to remember that this man holds both you and your mother in contempt. He's made it plain he believes Aunt Jess has been done out of her rights. So—what can you do to convince him otherwise?

CHAPTER TWO

FRUSTRATION gripped Fleur as the question rolled round in her mind, and, having explained the shortest route to the public hospital, she turned to him impulsively. 'Luke, would you please explain what you meant by saying Aunt Jess had been *done in the eye?*'

'Naturally, I meant the losing of her business to your mother.' The words were snapped crisply.

Fleur kept control of her temper. 'What makes you imagine the business belonged to Aunt Jess?'

He frowned as he stared ahead. 'Possibly because she always referred to it as *her* business, and to the loss of it being a real blow. I trust you'll grant me sufficient intuition to sum up the situation.'

Irritated, she stared at him gravely, her blue eyes shadowed by their dark lashes. 'I thought women were the people who possessed intuition. Men jump to conclusions and then refuse to admit themselves to be wrong.

His mobile lips twitched into a half-smile. 'You're an authority on men? No doubt you have numerous swains waiting in the wings.'

'I'm not completely neglected,' she flashed at him, vaguely needled by his amused tone and by the knowledge that several boyfriends had been in evidence until Craig Quinn had arrived on the scene to monopolise her evenings.

It had been her father's fault, she recalled peevishly. Take pity on the young chap, her father had requested when Craig had joined the law firm. He's lonely and a stranger in Palmerston North. But pity had betrayed her, because

Craig had continued to demand her company and she had
been too kind to refuse him. Other boyfriends had faded
into the background, although not one of them had
possessed the aura of magnetism that surrounded Luke
Riddell, nor could they compete with the virility that
seemed to ooze from him.

She liked his face and had become aware that the sound of
his deep voice stirred her senses. And despite the
undercurrent of antagonism simmering between them she
knew she would like to see more of him, although she
realised that further meetings would be unlikely. He had
said what he'd come to say, and Mother had given his
request the brush-off. Now he would return to Wanganui,
never to be seen again—at least, not by her.

His voice cut into her musings. 'I'm about to ask a favour
of you. I'd be grateful if you'd make an effort to persuade
your mother to think about spending a couple of days at
Rivermoon.'

'I'll try, but I can promise nothing, especially after your
very definite attitude of disapproval.' She paused to look at
him with eyes that were full of reproach then added, 'In any
case, I doubt that she'd have time. I don't suppose you have
any idea of the work entailed with flowers for a wedding.'

His shoulders lifted slightly. 'A bouquet for the bride?'

'And the bridesmaids—numerous flowers in the church,
large floral arrangements in the bride's home, shoulder
sprays for her mother and grandmother, buttonholes for all
the men involved . . .'

'OK, OK you've made the point. Your mother will
attend to the lot?'

'No. She'll have the help of two friends who are retired
florists and who love to assist on such occasions.'

'When is this wedding?'

'Next Saturday. So you can see that Mother can do
nothing, absolutely *nothing* about Aunt Jessica's Thursday

deadline.'

'Today is only Monday,' he pointed out. 'Surely she could give her Tuesday and Wednesday?'

Fleur smiled. 'Is persistence your second name? Are you always so determined about acquiring the things you want?'

'It's possible.' The reply came tersely.

The drive to the hospital took only a short time. The flowers were delivered and when they returned to the car she fastened her seat-belt, then sat waiting for him to switch on the ignition.

However, he failed to do so, and as he sat with his hands resting lightly on the wheel he said, 'You're sure I can forget the whole project?'

She sighed. 'I'm afraid so. There was a time when Mother would rush to do Aunt's bidding, but those days have long since gone.'

'What happened to cause the change? Perhaps you can tell me about it, or at least as much as you can remember.'

She looked at him doubtfully. 'Are you likely to believe me?'

'Try me. See if you can be convincing.'

'Why should I bother? Why should you be interested in anything I have to say, particularly when your sympathies are so very much with Aunt Jess? And let me tell you that Mother was well aware that you considered her to be in the wrong where Aunt Jess was concerned.' She paused, waiting for him to deny or excuse this fact, but he merely sat staring at her in silence.

At last he spoke quietly. 'I'd like to hear what you can remember of their relationship. It might throw some light on the cause of their quarrel.'

Another sigh escaped her. 'Really, Luke, I've no wish to talk about Aunt Jessica.'

'Not even in fairness to your mother? It would give me a veiw of her side of the situation.'

Fleur took a deep breath and said, 'In that case one word can tell you the cause of their trouble. Possessiveness. Absolute possessiveness on the part of Aunt Jessica.'

He assumed a bored air. 'No doubt that's what you were led to understand. Children are usually kept in the dark about matters that concern adults.'

She became impatient. 'There now, I *knew* you wouldn't believe me.' She glanced at her watch. 'Really, it's time you drove me back to the shop. Mother will be wondering. She knows where the hospital is and exactly how long it takes to deliver flowers.'

But he made no move to turn on the ignition. Instead he moved in his seat to face her, his eyes raking her features while the fingers of one hand stroked her cheek gently. 'Not so fast,' he said in a soothing voice. 'I'll take you back before very long. You can explain that I became stubborn and wanted to talk.'

'You mean you wanted to get me alone,' she accused with perception. 'You wanted to ask questions about our private affairs.'

'It's possible you can clear my mind concerning the shop's early days. I know that Jess is the elder sister, so I presume she started it and took your mother in at a later date.'

'Then your presumption is way off the beam, because they started it together. Their father set them up in it, giving each an equal financial interest, but this fact annoyed Aunt, who considered she should have the controlling interest. It was Aunt who decided the place should be known as the Fleurette.'

'So she was the boss,' he mused.

'Aunt was always the boss because she's a naturally bossy person. She threw her weight around, giving orders that were attended to by Mother, who ran right and left to do her bidding.'

'So there you are, Jess controlled the business.'

'Only because Mother allowed her to have her way in everything,' Fleur protested. 'Aunt is five years older than

Mother.'

'Then perhaps you can tell me what caused the rift between them. When did the real problems begin?'

'Does it really matter at this late date?' she asked, indicating her reluctance to go into further details.

'You've no wish to discuss it?' A hard note had crept into his voice.

'Not really.

His eyes became penetrating as their gaze held hers. 'In that case, your mother must have been at fault and you hate to admit it.'

The remark goaded her to say angrily, 'If you *must* know, Aunt was bitterly jealous because Mother had given birth to a baby when she herself had been unable to do so. And when Mother had the utter temerity to name me Fleurette after the florist's shop which Aunt considered to be her own, the trouble became worse.'

'It's possible she looked upon it as her baby. Wasn't she the one who did most of the work and carried the responsibility?'

'No doubt that's what she'd claim,' Fleur said, fighting to keep her temper under control. 'But Mother pulled her weight.'

'Didn't she have baby Fleurette to care for?'

'She was back at work as soon as possible. She brought me to the shop, and while she was busily making wreaths or bouquets I slept in my pram in the workshop.'

'A little flower among the flowers,' he murmured, his eyes examining her flawless complexion and the curve of her lips. 'It's a wonder somebody didn't take you home in mistake for a rose.'

'It pleases you to be sarcastic,' she flashed furiously.

'I really meant it as a compliment,' he returned quietly.

She looked at him in silence, again savouring his handsome features as she added, 'I'm afraid my name continued to be such a sore point with Aunt she refused to speak to Mother for almost a month. As for me, I'm told she'd hardly look at me.'

'And I can hardly believe a word you're saying.' A sudden harshness grated through his words.

Fleur caught her breath as she turned to send him a wide-eyed stare. 'You're a strange man, Luke Riddell. One moment finds you paying me a compliment, while the next finds you shouting that I'm a liar. As for believing me, you'll have to please yourself.'

His voice softened. 'At least I believe you must have been just like your name—a little flower.'

A flush crept into her cheeks, then it faded as the truth flooded her mind. 'You're laughing at me,' she accused angrily. 'You think my name is—is utterly *stupid*.'

'On the contrary, I think it's quite charming, but at the moment I'd like to hear more about the situation between your mother and her sister.'

'What's the use? You think I'm biased, *and a liar*.'

He ignored the latter accusation as he said, 'Of course you're biased. It's understandable. But apart from my own circumstances of needing my uncle's help, I have not yet heard sufficient reason for him to take Jess away from Palmerston North. There must be more to it. He must have had some very good reason for prising her away from the business she obviously considered to be her own.'

She looked down at her hands, wondering if she should tell him about the blow-up. Perhaps it would help him to understand why it was so unlikely that Mother would go rushing to Wanganui. That was if he believed her, of course.

Without looking at him, she said, 'As the years passed Mother continued to play the subordinate role. Everything that came into the shop was ordered by Aunt, and even when Mother tried to help with the accounts Aunt would take no assistance from her in that respect.' She paused reflectively. 'That was when Mother should have started to wake up.'

He sent her a sharp glance. 'Wake up? What do you mean?'

She ignored the question as she said, 'Despite their equal financial status Mother was like a servant, there to be given orders.'

'Didn't your father have anything to say about that particular state of affairs?'

'He was busy with his law practice, and Mother didn't complain because she preferred peace at any price.' She paused again before she said, 'This was the situation until the blow-up occurred.'

His eyes narrowed. 'What do you mean by the blow-up?'

'You haven't been told about it?' A peal of laughter escaped her, and for the first time she felt she had him at a disadvantage. 'Oh, yes, there was a blow-up and it had its repercussions.'

His mouth tightened with impatience. 'Suppose you tell me what it was about.'

'Once again it's possible you won't believe me, but if you want proof the records are all stacked in a cupboard in the workroom.'

'Go on,' was all he said, still watching her narrowly as he waited for her to continue.

'At the time it was quite frightening, and even now, after all the years, I can still see that man stamping into the shop. It was late afternoon and I'd come in from school. I always went straight to the shop after school——'

'And do you always take so long to get to the point or to relate an incident?' he cut in impatiently.

'Let me assure you it was more than an incident,' she retorted sharply, her eyes sparking with indignation.

'OK, so who was this man?'

'He was the accountant to whom the shop rent was supposed to be paid. He wanted to know why they were so far behind with it, and if something wasn't done right smartly they'd be out on their ears in a mighty short time. I can tell you it was a shock to Mother to learn the rent hadn't been paid for months.'

'So what happened? I presume it was paid.'

'More than that. My father stepped in and began to ask questions. He discovered that the business was over its head in debt because Aunt had mishandled the finances. Half the containers, potted plants and florists' necessities had never been paid for, and the place was overstocked with goods that were unlikely to sell.'

'It sounds as if the place was ready to go into liquidation.'

'That's it exactly. I can tell you that Uncle Bob was terribly upset. He tried hard to raise the money because the trouble had been caused by Aunt Jess.'

'I suppose it amounted to the tune of several thousand dollars?'

'It did. But he didn't have to raise a cent because my father came up with the necessary money.'

'And then things got back to normal?'

Fleur laughed. 'Not quite. You see, a change had occurred, and it was a change that did not please Aunt.'

'What do you mean?'

'Mother asserted herself.' Fleur's smile showed even white teeth as she uttered the words. 'When Daddy dragged them out of the red the money was paid on Mother's behalf, and this gave her a larger financial interest in the business. It also gave her the confidence she needed to stand up to Aunt Jess, and she became determined to have her say in the running of the Fleurette. In short, the worm had turned, and Aunt was not amused.'

'But no doubt she became used to the situation?' he queried.

'Not really, although she tried. Despite the severe knock to her ego, her natural possessiveness floated to the surface and within a short time she was making loud noises about having been robbed of what she considered to be rightfully hers.'

He laughed: 'Her baby had been snatched from her.'

'Something like that. Really, the situation was quite

ridiculous, but it didn't last for long because Uncle Bob
decided to move to Wanganui.'

'She went with him willingly?'

'I'm afraid not, but when he said he'd go alone she realised
she had little option but to accompany him.'

'Her share of the florist's shop not being worth a broken
marriage?'

'That would be right. Really, Luke, I'm tired of this subject.
May we talk about something else?'

'Just one more question,' he persisted. 'What happened to
her shares in the business?'

'Daddy bought them from her and put them in my name,'
she admitted with reluctance.

'So you're a part-owner in Fleurette.'

'Yes, and I'm afraid Aunt wasn't very pleased about *that*.
First I'd been given the name she'd chosen for the shop, and
then I'd acquired her own shares in it. Doesn't it tell you how
very much she resented me?'

He became thoughtful until he said, 'So these are the hard
blows she'd been dealt before coming to Wanganui.'

'It's the story as far as I can remember it. Whether or not
you believe it is another matter,' she added drily.

A cyncial smile hovered about his mobile lips. 'Let's say I
have my reservations.'

She turned upon him angrily. 'Are you suggesting I've
handed you a string of lies?'

'Not at all, but every schoolboy knows it takes two to fight,
but only one to hold out a friendly hand,' he remarked. 'And
as far as the Fleurette is concerned, your mother has now spent
ten years in the box seat, therefore she could afford to be
generous. It wouldn't hurt her to assist Jess for a couple of
days.'

'You don't give up, do you?'

'I mean just to complete the order due by Thursday. The
improved relations between them might enable Jess to cease

her bouts of ill-temper when she turns herself into a bag of misery and makes everyone else miserable as well, especially Bob.'

'That doesn't sound as if she's fretting over her relationship with Mother—at least I find it hard to believe.'

'That's because you're too young to understand that family ties become more important as people grow older. I'm sure she'd like the rift between her sister and herself to be healed and then——' He fell silent.

She turned questioning eyes upon him. 'Yes? And then?'

'Her attitude towards Bob might improve. Life might become easier for him. Every time she has one of her fretting bouts she takes it out on the poor old boy. She gives him hell.'

'How often do they occur?'

'Every time he goes to his club in the city. For heaven's sake, he's only spending a few hours with some of his cronies.'

'You're very fond of him,' she remarked, stating the obvious.

'Of course I'm fond of him. He's so like my father in appearance, and I hate to see the strained look on his face, the pained expression in his eyes.' His jaw tightened as he fell silent.

A sudden light dawned to clear her mind. Something about this man's concern for Aunt Jessica had failed to convince her, and while she had subconsciously groped for the reason she had failed to put her finger on it. But now it rose to face her, causing her to laugh.

'You find Bob's misery a joke?' he snarled.

'Not at all,' she chuckled. 'I merely find your cure for it amusing—quite funny, in fact.'

The dark brows drew together. 'Please explain yourself,' he demanded stiffly and without looking at her.

She turned to look at him squarely. 'The truth of the matter has only just clicked into my brain. It tells me you're not here on Aunt Jessica's behalf. Your whole purpose in coming here concerns Uncle Bob's peace of mind.'

'Well, maybe it's got something to do with it,' he admitted, still without looking at her.

'You've lived with Aunt Jess for ten years, therefore you know exactly what she's like and I doubt that you really care about her, or her Thursday deadline. But Uncle Bob's presence is like having your father back with you, and you loathe seeing him unhappy. Am I correct?'

'You're—surprisingly perceptive.'

'One doesn't have to be over-bright to understand how you feel about a man who is so like your father. It seems to me that you've caught on to the idea that a visit from Mother could possibly cause Aunt to change her attitude. She'd feel she's come out on top regarding the family quarrel, and Uncle Bob might not be made to feel so guilty every time he goes to his club.'

'Well, what do you think about it?'

'It *might* work, or it might *not* work, but one thing is certain—the family quarrel has gone on for long enough. I have only one aunt, and I do not like the fact that she and my mother do not speak to each other.'

'Do you agree it would not hurt your mother to be the first to hold out the hand of friendship? Do you think she could be persuaded to do it for Bob's sake?'

'I don't know. It's a pity you didn't explain the situation more fully to her. I mean about Uncle Bob. She might spare a couple of days for his sake.'

He switched on the ignition and revved the motor. 'Right. We'll return to the shop and I'll be more explicit,' he declared in a voice that betrayed hope.

As they left the hospital parking area she thought of Robert Riddell whom she recalled as being a patient, kindly man, a sort of underdog when compared with his domineering wife. Yet she felt sure that Aunt Jess had loved him. Or was her indomitable possessiveness stronger than her love? Was her attitude towards Bob still one which demanded that every minute of his spare time be spent at her side? Perhaps, if Luke explained this side of the situation to Mother, a small amount of help might be given.

But when they reached the shop this did not prove to be easy because Joyce was busily engaged with two customers who appeared to be a mother and daughter. Luke stood in the shop waiting for them to leave, but nobody seemed to be in a hurry and at last his impatience began to get the better of him.

'Do customers always take this length of time?' he gritted in Fleur's ear.

She hovered near the counter then returned to his side to whisper, 'It's possible they'll be ages. They're discussing the flowers for another wedding, going into costs.'

He glanced at his watch. 'In that case I'll have to rely on you to explain Bob's situation to your mother. Do you think you can do so?' He spoke with urgency, his dark grey eyes boring into hers as though demanding her compliance to his request.

'I'll try, but I can't promise anything in the way of results,' and as they reached his car which was now parked at the kerbside she added, 'I can understand Uncle Bob's reluctance about your visit to Mother. He was always a proud man.'

'Actually, it was Carla who suggested your mother might be persuaded to come. She felt sure it would make Jess happy.'

She turned to look at him. 'Carla? Who is she?'

'Jessica's housekeeper. She's a capable person who runs the house while Jess plays with flowers. She's a Miss Jensen. My parents knew her,' he added as an afterthought.

'I'm glad she has someone to help her,' Fleur said, the word 'capable' causing her to visualise a middle-aged woman, no doubt of ample proportions. 'She's always had a housekeeper?'

'This one has been with us for at least two years, but I'm afraid the others haven't stayed for very long periods.'

A thought struck Fleur. 'I'm surprised she hasn't trained Carla to help with the gift baskets.'

'She tried, but unfortunately she didn't like the results Carla produced. According to Jess she lacked the necessary flair, or perhaps she lacked imagination, therefore Jess decided she was more valuable attending to the house and preparing the meals. In any case, Jess is not always so far behind with her orders, but recently her arthritis has become more troublesome than usual.'

Fleur nodded with understanding. 'You're saying that this particular instance was sufficiently acute to give you the reason to call on Mother with a plea for help. And you're hoping that the help, if given, will lead to a reconciliation, which in turn *might* cure her bouts of fretting every time Uncle Bob goes to his club.'

He sent her a satisfied grin. 'That's about the sum total of the situation. I'm glad you've got the picture clearly in mind.'

'Except for one point. I'm still not convinced that Aunt's fretting is caused by family estrangement.'

'I can't think what else could be upsetting her.'

'And there's another point of which you are unaware, and that concerns Mother. During the last ten years she's become more like Aunt Jess by developing a strong determination. I think you'll have to be extra lucky to see her within yards of Rivermoon.'

His broad shoulders lifted in a slight shrug. 'Well, I've done my best. At least I've tried for Bob's sake.' He got into the car then spoke to her through the driver's window. 'I'll rely on you to persuade your mother to come. I need *her* and *nobody else*.' His words held a ring of command.

She laughed. 'You have to be joking when you imagine I can persuade Mother.'

He ignored the remark. 'Tell her to follow the River Road along the eastern bank of the Wanganui River. Rivermoon lies beyond the settlements.'

Fleur's face became serious as she issued a last warning. 'You'd be wiser to forget the whole project. I'm afraid Aunt's customer will just have to wait for the order to be completed in Aunt's own time. After all, gift baskets are not like wedding bouquets, which must be there at the right hour on the vital day.'

He made no reply although a shade of annoyance crossed his face as his hand reached towards the ignition key. And as the car glided away from the kerbside he spared her the briefest of nods as a gesture of farewell. Or was it a gesture of dismissal?

Watching the vehicle disappear round a corner, she felt vaguely frustrated by the suspicion that he had already forgotten her existence. Nor, she felt sure, would she ever see him again. So what did that matter? He was arrogant, overbearing, and expected everyone to jump to his commands. He had a gigantic nerve to expect Mother to drop everything and rush to Rivermoon—especially after Aunt Jessica had ignored them for ten years.

The utter temerity of the man left her almost breathless with indignation, and as she went back into the shop she told herself to forget him. Yet despite her efforts to wipe him from her mind his face continued to hover before her eyes, and within a short time she found herself making excuses for him.

He was kind and thoughtful, she reminded herself. He was one who would normally scorn to ask favours of anyone, of this she felt sure, yet he had come on behalf of the man who meant so much to him, the man who had taken the place of his father. Surely Mother would take these facts into consideration.

It was late in the afternoon before the subject could be broached, but eventually the time came when Fleur was able to say, 'Well, Mother, what do you think?'

Joyce turned to look at her. Pad in hand, she was checking the coloured ribbons arranged along their holding rod. 'What do you mean, dear? Do you realise we have another wedding coming up?'

'You know what I mean, Mother. This business about Aunt Jess.'

'Oh, *that*. If Jessica asks me for assistance I'll give it my consideration. Really, I had no idea we were so low on gold and yellow ribbons. The Meredith wedding is featuring autumn tones, so we'll need more.' She made a note on the pad.

'Are you going to do anything about it?'

'I'll order more, of course, and white as well.'

'I'm not referring to *ribbons*, Mother. I mean Aunt Jessica.'

'I know exactly what you mean.' She paused to make more notes, then sent a swift glance towards Fleur. 'Luke Riddell is quite handsome, don't you think?'

'I really didn't notice,' Fleur lied.

'Then we must get your eyes tested, dear. I thought him to be an agreeable young man.'

'At least he agrees with you on one point, Mother,' Fleur remarked in a dry tone.

Joyce's interest was caught. 'Oh? What would that be?'

'He thinks that life is too short to be clinging to quarrels—which is something you have declared almost every time we've made wreaths for funerals.'

Joyce remained silent, her mouth set in a stubborn line. It seemed obvious she knew exactly what Fleur meant but was not to be drawn.

Watching her, Fleur pursued, 'He came especially to ask for your help.'

'You mean he was *sent* to demand that I go crawling to Jess, but would *she* demean herself to ask for *my* help? Oh no, not likely.'

Fleur sighed. 'Mother, there's more to this situation than you realise. There's Uncle Bob to be considered. He's a dear person, and we were always fond of him.'

She made an effort to explain that Luke had really come on his uncle's behalf, and that a more cheerful Jessica could possibly make life easier for the man who had gone to help him when his father had died. Then, looking at Joyce wistfully, she added, 'So, not even for Uncle Bob's sake will you consider giving her a couple of days? You won't even *think* about it?'

Joyce was silent for several long moments before she said, 'You appear to feel very strongly about it.'

'Yes, actually I do. To be honest I'd like to see this family quarrel patched up.' She paused before saying eagerly, 'If you drive to Wanganui this evening you could give her all of tomorrow and Wednesday. I could manage here quite easily.'

Joyce smiled. 'You're rather sweet, Fleur. You're always so willing to help. Well, as it happens I've already come to a decision. I'm sending you in my place.'

Fleur was aghast. A quick breath escaped her as she gaped at her mother. 'You know very well they don't want me.'

'You could try to ascertain how deeply your aunt appears to be fretting. I doubt that you'll find the root of it stemming from the need for reconciliation with me.'

Fleur became conscious of a growing panic. 'Mother, Luke was *adamant*. He wants *you*—and nobody else. I wouldn't *dare* go in your place.'

'And that's another thing—you'll be given the opportunity to see him again.'

Fleur's tone became cool. 'How can you possibly imagine I have any wish to do so?'

Joyce laughed. 'Easily, because you're a sensible girl, and what sensible girl wouldn't want to see more of a man like Luke Riddell? He must be one of the most eligible young men in the district.'

'I am not looking for an eligible man,' Fleur snapped haughtily.

'Then it's high time you did,' her mother retorted. 'Now then, it's time we closed the shop,, and this evening you can pack a bag.'

The thought of going to Rivermoon in place of her mother almost gave Fleur a fit of the horrors. Grasping at straws, she said with urgency, 'No, Mother, I can't leave you with so

much work coming up—and—and there's the motel order for
the gift baskets.'

Joyce smiled. 'You're deliberately ignoring the extra
assistance I'm able to call upon, and you know very well that
we already have numerous gift baskets in stock. It'll be a
pleasure to supply Mrs Gordon so rapidly. Really, Fleur, I
expected you to jump at the opportunity to help poor Aunty.
And to meet Luke Riddell again,' she added with a side glance
at her daughter.

Fleur refused to look at her. 'I can assure you I'll not be
welcomed by either Aunt Jess or by Luke—especially not by
him. You are the one they're keen to see driving up to their
front door. He made that more than clear——'

'Nonsense,' Joyce cut in. 'They'll soon learn they've been
more than fortunate to have seen you arrive, particularly where
the gift baskets are concerned. You can leave first thing in the
morning.'

Fleur forced a smile to hide the dejection she felt. 'Mother,
has it never occurred to you that you're becoming exactly like
Aunt Jessica? More and more every day.'

Joyce sent her a startled glance. 'You mean I've
become—*bossy*?'

'*Very* bossy. Nor shall I leave first thing in the morning,
because you'll need me to be here while you go to see about
Mrs Gordon's dried arrangements,' Fleur reminded her.

'Yes, of course,' Joyce agreed in a brisk tone. 'Besides it's
always better to keep a man wondering.'

The remark brought a sharp rejoinder from Fleur.
'Mother—are you sending me to Aunt Jessica—or to Luke
Riddell?'

Joyce's smile was enigmatic. 'What do you think, dear?'

'Because if you have any matchmaking ideas in mind you
can forget them. You can think again.' Fleur's eyes flashed
with anger.

'Really, dear?' Joyce remained unruffled.

'Definitely. Nor do I like chauvinist males who fling their demands right and left and whose minds are closed to all but their own opinions. And believe me, in his opinion *you* are the only one who can help the situation at Rivermoon.'

CHAPTER THREE

IT WAS Wednesday morning when Fleur left for Wanganui. The April breezes blew in the partly open window as the small red Fiat sped north-westwards along the highway that crossed grassy plains. On either side the country presented a rural scene of timber-built homes and farm sheds nestling within the shelter of tree plantations. They were surrounded by herds of dairy cows, and flocks of sheep grazing green pastures that looked clean enough to have been freshly laundered.

Miles away to the right Mount Ruapehu rose from the North Island's high country, its snow-topped summit visible against the pale, clear sky, while to the left the distant views of fields were broken by extensive dark green shelterbelts of pines which gave protection from westerly winds sweeping in from the sea.

As Fleur drew nearer to Wanganui a sense of apprehension began to seep into her mind. She felt absolutely no joy at the thought of spending even a short time at Rivermoon, and now that she was on her way to the property she became conscious of mixed feelings that flipped from one aspect to another until she was almost on the verge of turning back towards home.

What sort of welcome could be expected from Aunt Jessica? Memory slid to her childhood years when she had always been more than a little afraid of her mother's sister, who had never made the slightest effort to show affection to anyone.

And then the thought of Luke almost make her quail. He

had come to ask for help from her mother rather than from herself, so what sort of reception could she expect from *him*? Would his grey eyes take on the glint of cold steel? Instinct warned that he would be annoyed because her mother had not seen fit to make the effort, and that the sight of her could only fill him with irritation.

In an attempt to brush away the sense of foreboding that grew stronger with every passing mile, she turned her thoughts towards her destination, then drew to the side of the highway to study her road map. The route to the River Road was clearly marked, and she could see there was no need to cross the bridge which would take her into the city and main area of Wanganui.

She put the Fiat into gear, and after a few more miles she had a view of Wanganui's Memorial Tower rising against the distant skyline. Although she knew that climbing it to see the extensive views was one of the things to be done when visiting the river city, she also knew she would not be making the effort because she had a strong dislike of heights. Even looking over a balcony was inclined to make her feel slightly uncomfortable.

A short time later, she took the turn that sent her along the river's eastern bank. The rising land on her right formed an eastern suburb where attractive homes lay beyond well-kept gardens, while on her left the broad, slowly flowing river made its way between tree-lined banks towards the Tasman Sea.

Driving beyond the residential area, she made her way along the valley towards open country where tall Lombardy poplars rose in stately lines. Their thick trunks were gnarled, and, already clad in autumn gold, they sent sprinklings of yellow leaves to the ground as she drove past.

Further along the valley more lines of poplars lifted branches towards the sky, and as she watched the sun glisten on the flutter of yellow leaves she almost missed the entrance to Rivermoon. A hasty foot on the brake brought the Fiat to a standstill, then she backed and turned to drive between sturdy pillars formed from smooth river boulders. Each pillar had extending stone walls, and the iron-barred cattlestop lying between them rattled as she drove across it.

The tree-bordered driveway crossing the front paddock formed an avenue of chestnuts, elms and oaks, and as she approached the two-storeyed white-timbered house she saw that the upstairs windows would give views of the river.

A circular lawn lay in front of the homestead, the drive following its circumference to enable easy exit back to the road. She noticed that the drive also branched to sweep round to the back of the house, but she stopped at the front door where an imposing portico sheltered the entrance.

For a few moments she sat hesitating, then she ran lightly up the wide concrete steps to press a bell set beside the doorway. She heard it echo in the distance, and after a short wait the door opened abruptly and she found herself faced by a young woman who appeared to be only a few years older than herself.

Hazel eyes with green flecks in them stared at Fleur from a round face framed by blonde shoulder-length hair. And while the face was pretty enough, its expression was ruined by a sulky mouth. And then the eyes narrowed slightly as they examined Fleur from head to foot, taking in every detail of her smart deep red woollen suit until the woman asked in a vaguely suspicious voice, 'Yes? What do you want?'

'I'd like to see Mrs Riddell, please. Is she in?'

'Yes, she's in—but she's busy in her workroom.'

Fleur forced a smile. 'Then could I see her, please?'

'What do you want?' The question came with cool abruptness.

'I've just told you. I want to see Mrs Riddell.'

'And I've just told you she's busy. You can state your business to me.'

But before Fleur could make a reply a voice came from the

end of the hall. 'Who is it, Carla?'

Carla? *This was Carla?* Fleur was startled. She had expected Jessica's housekeeper to be a more mature woman, the plump middle-aged person of her imagination in the age-group of Luke's parents.

'I think it's somebody selling something,' Carla called over her shoulder. Then to Fleur she said, 'Whatever it is, we don't want it.'

'We'll see about that.' Fleur forced another smile as she looked beyond Carla towards the woman who came into the hall. She recognised her aunt at once, and as Jessica came slowly nearer she could see changes such as ageing and extra weight. However, there was still a vague likeness to her mother, despite the fact that her aunt had brown eyes and a slightly darker complexion. The brown eyes now stared at her blankly until she felt compelled to say, 'It's Fleur, Aunt. Don't you recognise me?'

'*Fleurette*—my goodness, you've grown up.' Jessica's eyes darted to the Fiat parked at the bottom of the steps. 'Your mother—she hasn't come with you?'

'No. I'm afraid she's busy with weddings and other things, but she's able to get assistance so I was free to come.'

There was a silence until Jessica said, 'You've taken up floral work? You can't have been in it for very long.'

Carla put in, 'You really need someone with experience, Jess.'

Fleur ignored the remark as she spoke to her aunt. 'I've worked with Mother ever since I left school. Luke told us you needed help, so I've come to give you a few days. That is if you want me.'

'I really expected your mother to come,' Jessica complained in a petulant voice. 'Luke *promised* he'd do his best to persuade her,' she added, making no effort to hide her disappointment.

'I can assure you he did,' Fleur told her. 'However, if you don't want me I can go home at once.'

'No, please don't do that,' Jessica said hastily. 'You'd better come in. It's almost lunch time.'

'Very well.' She turned to fetch her suitcase from the car and in doing so she came face to face with Luke Riddell, who was coming up the steps. As they paused to stare at each other she became aware of the coolness in his attitude towards her. There was no smile of welcome, and, as she had feared, his eyes reminded her of cold steel.

He was the first to speak. 'So—your mother didn't see fit to come.' His voice held a hard ring that echoed her previous thoughts concerning his possible reaction.

Fleur looked at him steadily. 'Surely her reason was made clear enough to you.'

'Oh, yes—somebody's wedding, wasn't it?'

'I've already explained that there's a mountain of work and thought attached to the floral decorations for a wedding, to say nothing of the hassle of finding the right flowers. However, she did *see fit*—as you put it—to sacrifice the help I could have given her. Or is it not possible for you to appreciate that small fact?'

His expression became cynical. 'Perhaps it means that your own—er—expertise is not up to weddings.'

Fleur refused to allow herself to become ruffled, nevertheless she took a deep breath as she asked, 'Is that remark intended as a slur on my ability?' Then, glaring at him, 'I've already pointed out to Aunt that I can go home—*at once*.'

But before he could reply Jessica sent a reproachful look towards him. 'You *promised* me my sister would come.'

'I promised nothing,' he snapped at her. 'I merely told you to hope for the best.'

'The best, you say?' Jessica echoed with a short laugh.

He glared at her coldly, then almost snarled, 'Watch your tongue, Jessica, or you're likely to find yourself without the help that is now available.'

Jessica pulled herself together. 'Yes, of course—I'm very

glad Fleur has come. She might be able to do the gift baskets—quite nicely,' she added in a tone of concession.

'But without your own flair or imagination,' Fleur was unable to resist putting in, then she began to laugh as she added, 'Dear Aunt Jessica, you're still the same as you always were.'

'What's that supposed to mean?' demanded her aunt suspiciously.

'You're exactly as I remember you,' Fleur replied with an enigmatic smile. 'Perhaps you could show me where I'm to work and then I can get on with whatever has to be done. I think Luke said something about an order for gift baskets.'

'That's right. But before we go to the workroom Luke will carry your suitcase upstairs and then we'll have lunch. Bob will be in at any moment.'

Luke said nothing as he removed her case from the car, nor did he speak as he led her along the thickly carpeted hall towards a wide stairway rising from the end of it.

She followed him like an obedient child, and when they reached the upper passage she found herself being ushered into a guest-room that was complete with a bathroom en suite and a door leading out to the balcony.

He placed her case on a low stand then turned to regard her, and, apart from his eyes still being as cool as pebbles, his face was inscrutable.

She sensed that questions lurked within his mind, therefore she said, 'I can't help feeling that something is troubling you. I can only suppose you're disappointed because Mother hasn't arrived, but I did warn you that it was unlikely.'

'Disappointment has now been overridden by surprise,' he admitted tersely, his eyes taking in the cut of her smart red suit, her black shoulder bag and matching high-heeled shoes.

Her brows rose. 'You're surprised by the fact that I've come? Didn't you say Aunt needed help?'

'Yes, but after ten years and your previous poor relationship, why should it concern you? I mean, why should you bother to give it a second thought?'

She looked at him wordlessly. Indeed, why had she bothered? And as she searched her mind for an answer she refused to admit the truth even to herself. *You'd see Luke Riddell again*, her mother had said. And, while she had brushed the suggestion aside, honesty forced her to confess to herself that it had simmered at the back of her brain, quietly urging her towards Rivermoon.

His voice rang with irony as it cut into her thoughts. 'To be honest, I can't help wondering about you. Is it possible you've been endowed with a philanthropic nature? Are you a kind humanitarian who is generous to a fault, to say nothing of being utterly forgiving for past grievances on your mother's account?'

She gaped at him. 'What are you going on about?'

'Or is there some other reason that has drawn you towards dear Aunty? I mean, after all these years——'

She frowned, still trying to fathom his meaning, then shook her head in a helpless manner. 'I'm afraid I don't know what you're talking about. What are you trying to say?'

'OK, I'll try to be more specific.' He took several paces about the room, then stood still to face her, his voice becoming icy as he said, 'I can't help wondering if it's really your aunt's need for help that has brought you here.'

She looked at him with perplexity. 'That's a strange statement to hear, especially from you. Didn't you visit the Fleurette to ask for help—or is that something I dreamed up?'

'You didn't dream it, but help was requested from your mother, remember?'

She sighed. 'I hope we're not going over all that again.' Then, moving to the balcony door she stood staring across the fields to where a bend in the river could be seen. 'So what other reason could I have?' she asked at last.

A short laugh escaped him. It echoed derision. 'Indeed, what other reason?'

A sudden uneasiness gripped her, making her afraid to turn and look at him. Surely he couldn't have guessed that the real reason lay within his own handsome self—that despite her own mental denials she felt drawn towards him? If this were so she would die of embarrassment.

But his next words swept these fears from her mind. 'I can't help recalling my own careless words concerning your aunt's windfall,' he drawled.

She swung round to stare at him. 'What do you mean?'

His jaw hardened. 'I was even indiscreet to the extent of revealing its value.'

'Yes—so what?'

'Did it have anything to do with your decision to come here? Is it possible it urged you to offer whatever help you're capable of offering?'

It took several moments for the meaning of his words to register, and she almost felt her face turn pale as she gaped at him in speechless fury. At last she hissed, 'Are you hinting that I'm hoping to benefit from it in some way?'

His lips twisted. 'It's possible. After all, what else?'

She fought to control her temper. 'How *dare* you make such a—a horrible suggestion? The thought never occurred to me, but now that you've brought it up I can certainly see what's troubling *you*. It's as plain as the back of a bus.'

'Is that a fact?' he gritted. 'And what, may I ask, is troubling me?'

A mirthless laugh escaped her. 'Obviously you're afraid I'll cut in on you. If anything happened to cause my aunt's death, her—*windfall*—would probably be left to her husband, and no doubt it would go from him to you. Oh, yes, it's easy to guess you don't want to see me worming my way into my aunt's affections. Oh, no, not for one moment would you wish to see that happen.'

His eyes glittered angrily while his mouth became a hard, thin line. 'Why you—you wretched little——'

'Isn't gold-digger the term you're seeking?' she asked with forced sweetness. Then, allowing her eyes to examine him from head to foot, she added scathingly, 'You *look* like a fine example of the male species, Luke Riddell, but it's only on the outside. Inside you're not very nice at all. Your mind is full of rotten suspicion. Now if you'll excuse me, I'd like to wash my hands before lunch.'

He stood still, glaring at her in undisguised fury before he swung round and strode from the room.

Fleur felt shaken as she went into the en suite bathroom and turned on the washbasin taps. She knew she had scored the last word in this encounter, but it afforded her little or no joy, mainly because she was unable to believe her own accusations.

In her own heart she felt sure that Luke was not the type of man whose expectations revolved round an inheritance, nor did she really consider him to be horrible inside. Her words had been born of a desperate need to lash out and hit him, to hurt him in retaliation for his remarks. Gold-digger, indeed—and even if she herself had been the one to use the word it was the term he had in mind. Did he honestly believe she had come because of her aunt's wealth? The thought made her cringe.

A few rapid brush-strokes to her dark hair, coupled with an extra smoothing of lipstick, helped to calm her ruffled spirits, and as she gazed at her reflection in the mirror she was relieved to see that the flush of anger had faded from her cheeks. Get to work on those baskets, then head for home, she advised herself.

When she made her way downstairs the sound of voices drew her to what proved to be the living-room. Luke was there, leaning an elbow against the mantelpiece while chatting to an older grey-haired man who sat in an armchair. The latter stood up as she entered the room, and despite the passing of ten years she recognised him at once.

'Uncle Bob.' A glad smile broke over her face as she crossed the room to be hugged and kissed.

'Well, if it isn't Fleurette, the little flower all grown up. Let me look at those blue eyes. Shouldn't you be named Gentian or Delphinium?'

She laughed happily. 'Darling Uncle Bob, you're still the same big tease, but thank you for such a lovely welcome.'

'Haven't you had that already?' He frowned, then sent a questioning glance towards Jessica who emerged from the adjoining kitchen.

Fleur said hastily, 'Well, both Aunt and Luke were disappointed when I arrived instead of Mother.'

Jessica began to make excuses for herself. 'I'm afraid I was rather cross. I'd hoped—I really thought Joyce should have come.'

'Why? She owes you nothing.' Bob's voice rang with a hard note. 'But you'll notice she has at least sent her daughter.' He turned to Fleur. 'Why should Luke be disappointed? I'd have thought——'

Fleur's chin rose, her eyes widening with reproach as she turned to look at the man standing beside the mantelpiece. 'Oh, he's jumped to his own conclusions. He senses an ulterior motive in my arrival. I'm sure he'll be only too happy to supply you with details.'

'Ulterior motive—what damned rubbish is this?' Bob demanded, looking from Luke to Fleur.

There was a long pause while Fleur continued to gaze steadily at Luke, daring him to bring his former accusation out into the open and to lay it before his uncle and Jessica.

But he was not to be goaded into uttering his suspicions, perhaps because he realised that to do so would be sufficient to send her rushing back to Palmerston North at once. Instead he gazed at them coldly as he said, 'It's not important. We'll discuss it later. In the meantime I could do with a drink. Scotch for you, Bob?' He moved to a cabinet and lifted a decanter.

'Thank you. But if it's not important, why should it be mentioned at all?'

Luke ignored the question as he turned to Fleur. 'A sherry for you, or something stronger?'

'Stronger? No thank you, I never take anything stronger than a medium sherry, if you have it.'

'Of course I have it. I keep it for Carla. Incidentally, your keys were left in your car. I've parked it in one of the sheds.'

'Thank you—it won't take up space for very long.'

He ignored the remark as he turned to her aunt. 'Jessica? You'll have a drink?'

'You know I'm not supposed to have alcohol,' Jessica complained petulantly, then she straightened her shoulders and added in a defiant tone, 'I'll have a Scotch this time. It might make me feel more cheerful.'

'And less disappointed in my arrival,' Fleur laughed, determined to make light of the situation.

She then turned to watch Luke pour the drinks, and as she did so she observed the tightness about his mouth and jaw. She also sensed his underlying irritation, and as he offered her a stemmed crystal glass of golden liquid she became aware of the icy glitter in the grey eyes that seemed to be intent upon piercing her mind.

It was then that a feeling of anticlimax gripped her. Was this the man who had drawn her to Wanganui? Was he the same person whose acquaintance she had been anxious to further? She must have been daft, and suddenly she was obsessed by a strong urge to go home, to be away from him and his suspicious mind. As the desire became more intense Bob's voice pierced her thoughts.

'How long can you stay with us, Little Flower?' he asked, using the name he had given her during her childhood.

The memory of it brought a faint smile to her lips, and she then became conscious that all eyes were resting upon her. Jessica's held hope, while Luke's were plainly mocking. She stared into her glass thoughtfully, but before she could form a reply Jessica's voice echoed with confidence. 'Fleurette has promised to stay for at least a fortnight.'

The temerity of the statement almost took Fleur's breath away. 'I made no such promise, Aunt,' she protested. 'It hasn't even been discussed yet.'

Bob chuckled. 'The Scotch has gone to her head. It's brought on a bout of wishful thinking.'

'Nothing of the sort,' Jessica snapped at him. 'It's just that there are so many baskets to be done.'

'Why not let Fleur speak for herself?' Luke drawled on a cynical note. 'She might like to stay for a month—or even longer.'

She turned to look at him, and perhaps it was the sight of the sardonic expression still lurking about his mouth that made her say, 'I shall not be staying at all. I'll have lunch with you and then I'll spend the afternoon in Aunt's workroom. At five-thirty I'll leave for home.'

A wail of protest escaped Jessica. 'My dear, you can't give me much help in that short time.'

'Possibly not, but it's not my help that you really want,' Fleur returned calmly. 'That particular message has hit me with a loud bang, therefore I'm afraid you'll just have to tell your client you've been unable to complete the order by the required date.'

'But you came intending to stay,' Jessica reminded her. 'Luke carried your case upstairs.'

'That's right, and we had a most interesting chat while we were up there,' Fleur told her aunt, then as she turned to face Luke she realised the sherry was making her feel slightly uninhibited. Sherry was inclined to have that effect on her, but before she could say anything further a wail escaped Jessica.

'Well, really, I can't understand why you bothered to come at all if that's the only time you can spare me,' she declared crossly.

Fleur was still feeling talkative. She began, 'I'm sure Luke will help you to——' then broke off as Carla pushed a laden trolley through from the kitchen.

The blonde woman appeared to sense the tension in the air. 'Is everyone ready for lunch?' she asked doubtfully.

'More than ready, thank you Carla,' replied Luke swiftly. 'This sherry is for you.'

'Oh, thank you, Luke, you always remember to pour a sherry for me, and you know what I like.' She took the glass from him, her eyes glowing as she looked up into his face.

'Well, let's sit down,' Jessica said impatiently.

The two men took their places at either end of the table while Fleur was placed beside Jessica. Carla, on the opposite side, lifted the lid from a large tureen and began to serve an appetising soup. It was followed by a savoury dish of macaroni cheese, tomatoes and other tasty additions, and later came tea and date scones.

During the meal Bob made a valiant attempt to lighten the atmosphere by chatting to Fleur. 'Does your mother still grow most of her own flowers for the shop?'

'Yes. A man comes every Wednesday to do the garden. We now have a large area planted with immortelles.'

Carla looked at her curiously. 'Immortelles? What are they?'

Fleur looked across the table at her. 'I suppose most people call them everlasting flowers.'

Carla uttered a laugh that held a slight sneer. 'But you think "immortelles" displays your knowledge. I suppose, if the truth's known, you're merely in the early throes of learning floral work.'

Fleur smiled. 'One can always learn. I doubt that I'll ever stop learning.'

Jessica sent her a sharp glance. 'I hope you're not just a beginner on gift baskets?'

Fleur looked down at her plate, finding difficulty in concealing her amusement. 'I've attended a couple of courses in dried-flower arrangements. Mother thought it would be a good idea.'

Carla looked at Jessica, her eyes brimming with sympathy. 'I can understand why you were so keen for her *mother* to come.' She turned to Fleur again, probing to learn the extent of her knowledge. 'I don't suppose you know anything about the Japanese form of floral art. I—I forget what it's called.'

'Ikebana. I'm told it means the living flower. Its basic form usually follows the fixed pattern of a triangle representing earth, heaven and man. Emphasis is placed on linear perfection, space, form and colour harmony. However, I'm afraid I haven't the time to go into all its details because I'm anxious to make a start in the workroom. I'd like to do as much as possible before I leave.'

Her words were met by a silence until Luke spoke. During the conversation his eyes had rested upon her with questions lurking within their depths, causing her to remember his former accusations, and it seemed obvious that he still doubted her integrity, therefore his comment came as a surprise.

Looking at her gravely, he said, 'I'm beginning to suspect that you know more about floral work than we realise.'

'*Really*? Well, that's most generous of you. In fact it's quite *big* of you.' Fleur's face remained unsmiling.

The dark brows drew together. 'Why do you say that?'

'Because it's clear you've assumed I know nothing at all,' she retorted coldly.

Bob offered an excuse for Luke. 'Do you feel he's been underrating your ability? It's probably because you look so young.'

Jessica said hastily, 'I don't doubt your ability, dear. I recall that even before we came to Wanganui you'd begun making little posies. Do you remember the day your first posy was sold in the shop? We were all so excited.'

Fleur said nothing as she looked back to that day of her first sale. She had been eleven at the time and she had come to the shop to sit quietly making a posy in the workroom. When it was finished she had shown it to her mother who had put it on display among other posies created by Jessica and herself.

A short time later a customer had entered the shop. The posies had been examined, and the one picked up and carried to the counter had been the posy made by Fleur. She recalled that Mother had been excited, but Aunt Jessica had been scathing about a poor fool who had paid good money for a posy made by a *child*.

Brushing the memories aside she finished her cup of tea then stood up and said, 'If you'll show me your workroom, Aunt, I'll see what I can do before I leave.'

Bob put in a sly remark. 'Don't you mean you'll jolly well show us all that you can do more than we imagine?'

She made no reply as she followed Jessica through the kitchen and into a short passage. A door at the end of it gave an exit to the back yard, while a room leading off it proved to be the workroom. And this, apart from its disorder, was similar to the workroom at home, except that the pink, blue and yellow statice, the orange Chinese lanterns, the creamy dried bells of Ireland and the straw flowers hung from easily accessible racks instead of from the ceiling as in the Palmerston North shop.

Nor would the disorder on the workbench be tolerated at the Fleurette, and as she looked at the jumble of empty gift baskets, the rolls of ribbon, bundles of fine wire and blocks of Oasis, Fleur's instinct for orderliness urged her to do something about them. 'You are still the same, Aunt,' she remarked with a smile.

'Are you saying I'm still as untidy as ever?' The question came sharply. 'Does it not occur to you that reaching to put things back on shelves hurts my shoulders? I'm in pain, do you understand?'

Fleur tried to make amends. 'I—I meant you're still the same person who works on several projects at the same time.'

'Oh. Well, believe me I'm not the same person at all,' Jessica retorted crossly. 'Just look at my hands. Manipulating the secateurs and the wiring of stems nearly kills me.' She thrust hands with swollen knuckles towards Fleur. 'Just look at my fingers. I'm fast reaching the stage when I'll be unable to cope. And now you've brought me some help, but you're taking it away almost at once,' she finished on a plaintive note.

Fleur looked at her in silence. How could she explain that her decision to leave had been caused by Luke voicing his suspicion that she had come merely for her own gain? The knowledge that he considered her to be nothing more than an opportunist had got under her skin. It had pierced her pride, and even as she recalled the stinging contempt ringing in his words she became conscious of a renewed surge of anger.

And then, looking at her aunt's painful hands, pity overrode her anger. After all, why should she care about Luke Riddell's opinion of her? He could criticise her till his eyes struck fire. He could imagine the worst of her, she couldn't care less, and it was sympathy for Jessica's plight that made her say, 'Well, if you approve of my work, perhaps I could stay for a couple of days.'

'My dear, I'd be so grateful,' Jessica quavered. 'In that case you'd better come and see my main stock of everlastings. They're out in a shed that Luke has put at my disposal.'

She led the way through the door at the end of the passage and towards a small building situated near the house. Inside were inverted bunches of flowers, hanging to dry until they were ready for use, and a rapid glance showed the variety to be extensive.

'Bob grows them for me,' Jessica said with a satisfied air. 'He's developed an area on the shaded side of the garden so that the sun doesn't fade the flowers before they're picked. Colours are always more intense when grown in a cooler area. I'll show you where it is.'

They left the shed to follow a path leading towards the south side of the house where numerous immortelles still waited to be gathered, and as Jessica examined them critically she said, 'Some of them are almost ready to be picked——'

Fleur felt a surge of impatience. 'Yes, but really, Aunt, I'd like to get on with the job. If you'll just let me loose in the workroom I'll make a start. I understand the order must be completed by Thursday, which is tomorrow.'

'By early Thursday afternoon to be exact.' Luke's voice spoke from behind them, the unexpected sound of it causing Fleur to jump. He had followed them along the path and now regarded her ironically. 'If it's possible for you to give any assistance at all, why not get cracking and do so? I mean, five-thirty is only a few hours away.'

'Aunt was merely showing me where extra flowers can be found,' she flashed at him coldly. 'Or are you afraid I'm making a quiet attempt to get closer to her——?' She stopped abruptly, appalled by the words this man was capable of forcing from her. Turning to Jessica she said, 'If you'll excuse me, Aunt, I'll go to the workroom.' And without another glance at Luke she hurried indoors.

She was still feeling mentally shaken when she began sorting the workbench. Unnecessary items were almost thrown to a shelf, leaving only the materials she would need, and as she began to choose an assortment of baskets Jessica's voice came from the doorway.

'Have you found everything you want?'

'Everything except the main supply of Oasis.'

'It's in a box beneath the bench.' Jessica hesitated before asking, 'Is there something wrong between you and Luke? I've told him you've agreed to stay for a couple of days.'

Fleur made no reply as she found the box of Oasis, then extracted blocks of the dense sponge-like plastic foam which would support the stems she pushed into it. 'Are these the baskets you had in mind?' she asked, still ignoring any reference to Luke.

Jessica examined them critically. 'Yes, they'll be suitable. I always make an array of different sizes. Perhaps I'd better leave you to get on with it. You won't want me peering over your shoulder.'

Fleur couldn't agree more, therefore she remained silent and moments later she heard the door close behind her aunt. She then chose her first basket and sliced a piece of Oasis to fit into its base. This had to be anchored to the wickerwork by using green adhesive tape, and with it safely secured she turned to survey the everlasting flowers at her disposal.

After that the time passed with surprising speed and by mid-afternoon she was working on her third basket. The narrow ribbon she curled by running a blade along its length sprang into a spiral tail, and as she placed it carefully she heard the door open.

Aunt had returned to see her progress, she thought, without turning round, and she drew in a long slow breath as she awaited the comment which would surely contain criticism. But Jessica's voice did not sound in her ears, because it was Luke who walked into the room.

Wondering why he had come, she decided to ignore him, and after a brief glance over her shoulder she continued to work in silence, attaching ribbon bows to looped wires which could be pushed into the Oasis foam.

He observed her expertise for several long moments before he said with a hint of surprise, 'I presume you've done this before.'

She straightened her back. 'You do? I don't find that so amazing I mean, you're so good at *presuming*.'

He ignored the taunt while continuing to stare at the two completed baskets. 'They remind me of the ones in the Fleurette. Is it possible they were made by you, rather than by your mother?'

'It is possible,' she retorted tersely.

'Why didn't you tell me you'd made those baskets.'

'Because you were pleased to *presume* otherwise. You gave

me the impression you thought I was the prize simpleton about the place, perhaps capable of putting a few blooms into a bouquet, taking cash over the counter and making the tea. In actual fact I've been making gift baskets for years. It's my special department at the Fleurette.' She paused to control her irritation, at the same time wondering why she allowed this man to get under her skin.

'Are you saying my opinion is important to you?' The question came softly, almost as though reading her thoughts.

'Certainly not. Your previous remarks have proved your opinion to be unworthy of a second thought,' she flared, irritated further by the suggestion. At the same time she realised he had moved to stand closer to her, and, gripped by a sudden nervous tension, her fingers trembled as she poked a bronze straw flower into the Oasis. Then, deciding it was too small for that particular position, she whipped it out again.

'Am I making you nervous?' he asked mockingly.

'Not at all,' she lied, feeling her tension grow stronger. 'But I'll admit I hate people watching while I work. Even Mother knows better than to do so.' There now, that should tell him to go away, she thought.

But the words had no such effect, and instead of taking the hint he said, 'I suggest you stop work and listen to what I have to say.'

'I'm not really interested, especially if it concerns my reason for being here.'

'I've merely come to say thank you.'

'Thank you? For what?'

'For not rushing home immediately, as you'd threatened at the table. Jess said you'd changed your mind and would at least complete this order for her, which means you'll stay a couple of days.'

She paused in the act of snipping a stem, then laid the serrated scissors on the bench as she turned to face him, her eyes wide from an inner hurt. 'No doubt it gives you much satisfaction. It must confirm your suspicions regarding my motive for coming here.'

His expression became indecipherable. 'Only time will show results from the fact that you've come.'

'Don't you mean that only time will show proof of your accusation?'

'I can see that it really got to you.'

'*Got to me*? Never in my life have I felt so insulted.'

'You're admitting to being somewhat thin-skinned?'

'No, I am not, and what's more I'd be grateful if you'd stop hindering me. I'll finish this job and then get to hell out of your house.' A sudden rush of tears blurred her eyes. She blinked at them angrily as she turned back towards the workbench.

'Never to set foot in it again?' he queried with a soft laugh.

'That's right,' she stormed at him. 'And I'd take it as a favour if you'd keep away from the Fleurette.'

'You're making the remainder of your stay here very difficult,' he pointed out, his voice losing its mocking note. 'Jess will be upset if she knows we're at loggerheads. Would it not be possible to call a truce for the short period? Or are you so boiled up with your own injured feelings that her sensibilities don't matter a hoot?'

'Of course they matter, and I feel sorry to see her suffering from those wretched arthritic pains. Very well, we'll call a truce. It need last for only as long as it takes me to finish these baskets, and then we'll say *goodbye*!'

But even as she almost shouted the last word she became vaguely conscious of a doubt at the back of her mind.

CHAPTER FOUR

LUKE uttered a soft laugh. 'Good girl,' he said. 'And then there will be no need for us to set eyes on each other again—ever.'

She stared at him dumbly, aware that this was not what she wanted at all. But how could she put it into words?

His hands on her shoulders turned her to face him again, the action being gentle and unhurried while he stared down into her face. His voice held a deeper tone than usual. 'Do you know that anger makes you look vibrant? Your cheeks are rosy, your eyes are flashing. Your mouth is so very provocative—I've a good mind to kiss it.'

'You wouldn't dare——' she gasped. But instead of shrugging herself free from the grip that sent fire shooting through her veins she continued to gaze up into his face like a paralysed dove held in a conjurer's hand.

'Dare is the wrong word to use with me,' he said quietly, lowering his head to brush her lips with his own. 'However, I'd just like to say thank you for deciding to stay.' The words came as a murmur, his mouth remaining only inches away.

Wordlessly, she looked up into the dark grey eyes that held an indefinable glitter, and as his fingers bit into her shoulders she found herself pulled against his broad chest. Again his mouth descended upon hers, this time with a force that held more meaning, and despite her eforts to whip herself into a state of fury she found herself unable to think clearly. Instead, her senses reeled before leaping into a dizzy state where it was impossible to do other than respond with helpless ardour.

As the kiss ended she pushed herself free of his arms. Her

face crimson, she demanded, 'Do you always say thank you in that manner?'

There was a long pause before he said with a huskiness in his voice, 'As you were saying, you'd better get on with the job. I don't wish to hinder you by starting all over again, although it's very tempting.

'*I'll bet it is.*' Carla's words held the lash of a whip as, pale-faced, she stood watching them from the open doorway. Her icy voice continued with bitter sarcasm as she said, 'Pardon me for interrupting this—this amorous interlude—but Jess has sent me to tell you there's tea being poured in the living-room.'

'Thank you, Carla.' Luke's reply came nonchalantly. It was almost as though being caught in the act of kissing a girl was an everyday occurrence and nothing to cause surprise. 'We'd better go,' he added to Fleur. 'I'm sure you could do with a cup of tea.'

Could she ever! She followed him meekly, hardly daring to glance at Carla, whom she sensed to be oozing suppressed fury, and as she entered the living-room she was thankful to see that Bob was already there, sipping his tea. Dear Uncle Bob, she thought. Somehow he always seemed to bring things back to normal. Even in the old days he usually had a soothing effect when things became difficult with Aunt Jessica.

And now Jessica became full of anxious queries which she directed at Fleur. 'How are you getting on, dear? You'll notice I've kept out of the workroom, although I was very tempted to make sure you were wiring each of the small stems.'

'Of course, Aunt, and taping them as well. I wouldn't neglect those basic rules.'

Carla put in a sly remark. 'You needn't worry, Jess. Luke has been acting as overseer. Very successfully, I'd say.' The look she sent him was filled with reproach.

'He was there for only a few minutes,' Fleur protested without daring to look at Luke.

'Such delightful minutes,' Carla remarked with a brittle

laugh.

'I was merely saying thank you,' Luke put in mildly.

'Of course—who could imagine you'd be saying anything else.' Fleur flashed at him, then felt annoyed for having uttered the remark. To cover her embarrassment she turned to Jessica and said, 'Yes, Aunt, to be frank I do prefer working alone, unless I happen to be doing the preparation task of wiring and taping the stems, and even then I like to concentrate because it's the preparing that's so important to the end result.'

'I know what you mean,' declared Jessica firmly. 'In that case you must not allow Luke to hinder you. You've a lot to do in a short time.'

Carla's lips thinned as she spoke with a hint of scorn. 'I don't think Fleur will really mind being—*hindered*.'

The bitterness in the blonde's tone sent questions leaping into Fleur's mind. Was there a reason for Carla's objection to her being kissed by Luke? Was there an understanding of some sort between them—or did Carla merely have hopes of a closer association?

She turned to look at Luke, wondering if the remark and its revealing resentment had caught his ear, but apparently it had gone unnoticed because he had become involved in a discussion with Bob. Listening, she heard snippets of conversation concerning the amount of hay in the barns and the supply of winter feed already in hand for the stock, and it was with a sense of relief that she doubted that Carla's remark had even registered with him.

Feeling more at ease, she drank her tea quickly then stood up and placed her cup and saucer on the table. 'Thank you for the tea, Aunt—now I'll go back to the workroom.'

Jessica rose stiffly. 'I'm coming to see what you've been doing. I really can't stay away any longer.'

They left the room and moments later Fleur stood waiting for the criticism she knew must come. But to her amazement her aunt's approval betrayed a mixture of pleasure and surprise.

'My dear, I had no idea you could make them so professionally. They're quite beautiful. Elaine Barker will be delighted.'

'Thank you, Aunt.' Jessica's surprise caught her to smile inwardly. 'Who is Elaine Barker.'

'She has a florist's shop in town, but she's so busy with other things she hasn't time to spend on baskets. Would you prefer to continue working alone, or would you like me to help with wiring stems? I'm afraid I can't work fast.'

Fleur thought rapidly. Despite her preference for working alone, she realised that her aunt's presence could prevent a further visit from Luke. She had no wish for more amorous advances from him, she tried to assure herself, therefore she said, 'Please help if you wish, Aunt, but I'll select the flowers to be used.'

The remainder of the afternoon saw them working side by side, this being something which a week ago Fleur would have thought to be impossible. And now, watching from the corner of her eye, she realised that the arthritis in her aunt's fingers had indeed become a problem.

At last Jessica sighed as she laid a flower on the bench. 'I'm afraid my days at this work are numbered, but I'll keep at it for as long as I can,' she said with a touch of her old determination. She stood up, her movements stiff as she left the stool, then she added, 'Perhaps I'd better see what Carla's doing about dinner.'

'She's been with you for a long time?' asked Fleur casually as her nimble fingers twisted the green florist's tape.

'Long enough to have become part of the place. She knows exactly what Luke likes to eat and places it before him. And heaven alone knows how I'd run this large house without her, despite the woman who comes to do the laundry work and clean the floors. I'll admit I've been wondering if she and

Luke——' Her words faded away.

'Will get married?' Fleur supplied, her interest quickening. 'Are there any signs of it?'

Jessica pursed her lips doubtfully. 'None that I've noticed, although I suspect Carla is keen enough. And who wouldn't be? One has only to look at him and all he has to offer. She'd be a fool to turn him down—that's if he asks her, of course.'

'She'd be a fool to marry him if she doesn't love him,' Fleur retorted, then became aware that her aunt was regarding her in a speculative manner.

'What do you think of him, my dear?' Jessica whispered.

The unexpected question startled. '*Me*? I've been too busy to give him a second thought.' Which was a lie, because ever since the tea-break she'd been having difficulty in brushing away the memory of his arms holding her against his chest and the feel of his lips on her own. Even the thought of his fingers biting into her shoulders sent a quiver down her spine.

Jessica said, 'We have pre-dinner drinks at six-thirty while we watch the television news. Be in the living-room by then.'

Fleur nodded, feeling relief when her aunt left the room, taking the subject of Luke and Carla with her. She worked rapidly until almost six o'clock, by which time she had made a start on her sixth basket, then she ran upstairs to change into something other than the red suit she had been wearing all day.

A quick shower removed some of the fatigue caused by bending over her work, and the coral-pink dress she put on suited her to perfection. It contrasted with her dark brown hair and sent a faint glow into her clear complexion, and as she took extra care with her make-up she told herself she wasn't applying these touches of eye-shadow for *him*. Oh, no, definitely not. His opinion meant nothing—nothing at all.

Then she sighed as she decided to stop fooling herself. She *was* trying to look attractive for Luke Riddell, and she might as well admit it, at least to herself, she thought, picking up a coral-pink lipstick. And it was as she smoothed it over her softly generous mouth that she heard a light tap on the door.

Her heart skipped a beat. Could it be Luke? Had he come to make sure she would be down for the six-thirty drinks, or for some other reason? A quick glance in the mirror satisfied her, but when she opened the door she found herself faced by Carla.

The blonde carried towels across her arm. 'I hope there were towels in this room,' she said politely as though making sure of this fact while her eyes took in Fleur's appearance.

'Yes, thank you.' Fleur looked at Carla curiously, instinct telling her that the towels had been used as an excuse to come and talk to her, and this proved to be correct when Carla walked further into the room.

She came straight to the point. 'Is he someone special to you?' she demanded abruptly, her voice full of suspicion.

Fleur was taken aback. 'Pardon? Who do you mean?'

'I mean Luke, of course, as you darned well know.'

'I must say your temerity amazes me,' Fleur retorted coldly, then added a counter question. 'Is he someone special to you?'

'Well, yes, he is. We've almost come to an understanding, so when I saw him kissing you I felt I had to know the truth.' Carla glared at her with cold hostility.

'Then you can believe it was nothing more than his way of showing gratitude,' Fleur assured her. 'Didn't he tell you he was merely saying thank you?'

'Thank you—for what?' Carla demanded with a hint of disbelief.

'For deciding to stay and help Aunt with the order, of course.'

'He's never shown gratitude to me in that manner, and I've done plenty for her,' Carla snapped crossly. 'How long do you intend to stay here, soaking up appreciation from Luke?'

Fleur ignored her rude tone. 'Who knows?' she smiled with a slight shrug. 'Maybe two days, maybe two weeks.' The latter statement amazed even herself. She had no intention of staying for two weeks, yet by doing so she could build up a backlog of stock for her aunt. And then honesty forced her to admit that she would also become better acquainted with Luke Riddell. Not that this would be her main reason, of course, and to prove this point to herself she made an effort to overlook Carla's unmistakable hostility. 'Have you known Luke for a long time?' she asked in a friendly tone.

'Of course. His mother was very fond of me. Actually I always felt she'd chosen me for——' The words trailed away.

'Really? You mean for Luke?'

'Naturally.' Carla tossed her head in an arrogant manner. 'You needn't think I'm just a servant in this house. I'm much more than that. I really belong in it and I don't intend to leave it—if you get my meaning,' she added with a defiant glare.

'The message is clear enough,' Fleur commented drily.

'So if you have any ideas concerning Luke you can forget them.'

'What makes you imagine I could have—ideas?'

'Well, you weren't exactly showing much protest. I saw no struggling from his arms, or slapping of his face.'

'I told you, he was merely saying thank you,' Fleur reminded her, then added thoughtfully, 'At the same time I must say you're taking a long time to make your position permanent?'

'All in good time,' said Carla loftily.

'Luke doesn't strike me as being one who would waste time. I suspect the girl he loves will find a ring on her finger in a very short time.'

Carla's eyes glistened. 'His mother had a beautiful ring. I wonder where it is.'

'Perhaps you'd see it sooner if you gave him a little competition,' Fleur suggested gently. 'Sally, who lived next door to us, was in love with a man who was satisfied with just coasting along without a word about marriage. Her mother advised her to look elsewhere, so she started going out with somebody else. It worked and they're now married with three children.'

Carla's attitude became haughty. 'I don't have to use those tactics with Luke, although actually there is somebody who has been asking me to go out with him. Next time I'll not be so stand-offish. It might make Luke jealous enough to—to——' She licked dry lips as her voice trailed away.

'To come to heel?' Fleur supplied with a laugh.

'Well, whatever,' Carla snapped. 'So kindly remember you're nothing more than Jessica's assistant in this house—and keep away from Luke,' she finished warningly.

Fleur ignored the last remark. She went downstairs, and as she entered the living-room Luke stood up. The navy shirt and fitting trousers he wore clung to his body, outlining the contour of long legs and muscled thighs, and doing nothing to conceal the virility of his athletic form.

He regarded her appearance for several moments before moving to the drinks cabinet where he poured her a sherry. Handing it to her, he murmured in a low voice, 'The bracket light above your head makes your hair shine like polished walnut.'

She was amazed to receive the compliment but managed to turn it aside with a light remark. 'Thank you—it's only a matter of work with the hairbrush.'

She then became aware of his eyes examining her face, resting on her lips before travelling slowly towards her throat where the low V-neck of her dress fell open from its mandarin collar. A flush stole into her cheeks as she forced her eyes to leave his face, turning to the doorway as Bob came into the room.

She noticed that he also had changed, and was surprised to see that his attire was even more formal than Luke's, his grey suit being relieved by a cream shirt, green tie and matching breast-pocket handkerchief. It caused her to wonder if he had dressed to this extent because she was there, but this thought was immediately dispelled by Jessica's resigned tones.

'You're going out—*again*, I see.'

Bob moved towards the drinks cabinet. 'Yes, m'dear. I'm going to the club to see the final of the billiard matches.' He paused, then added with a note of defiance, 'I might also join in a game of bridge.'

Jessica's lips thinned. 'What time will you be home?'

'When it suits me, m'dear. Or are you hoping to put a time limit on me?'

Jessica sniffed. 'Sometimes I wonder if that club means more to you than your wife.'

Bob grinned as he remarked calmly, 'Of course not, my dear one. It's merely a place where I can find pleasant companionship, and where nobody nags or jumps down my throat for no reason.'

Fleur noticed he remained in a jovial mood during dinner, and a short time later he disappeared. She also sensed that Jessica was curbing her ill-humour only with difficulty, while Luke offered the odd remark to placate her.

However, she was more concerned with the numerous glances Luke continued to send towards her face, and she couldn't help wondering what thoughts lay behind his veiled expression. Something appeared to be on his mind, but it did not emerge until later when she was helping Carla clear the table and stack plates into the dishwasher.

He came into the kitchen and looked about him. 'Has anyone seen the evening paper?' he queried.

Carla said, 'I don't think Bob brought it in. He must have forgotten.'

Luke explained to Fleur, 'It's thrown from a car that passes the road entrance. Would you like to walk with me to collect it?'

'You mean down that long dark avenue of trees?'

His lips twitched. 'Are you afraid of the dark? I could find a torch, although the paper is usually easy to find without one, especially in full moonlight.'

She glanced at Carla in time to see naked resentment flashing from the greenish hazel eyes, and while one part of her mind urged her to go with Luke, the other part shouted caution while bringing back the memory of his earlier embrace. It would be like asking for a repeat performance, and as this was something for which she was not yet ready she forced a smile and said, 'Why not take Carla for a walk instead of me?'

His expression hardened. 'I was under the impression I'd asked you. Are you saying you've no wish to walk along the drive with me?'

Suddenly torn by indecision, she hesitated before saying, 'It's—it's just that I have a job of wiring to do.'

A scowl crossed his face. 'You're insinuating that Jess is a slave-driver?'

'Of course not, but you must understand that it's the wiring and taping of stems that's so time-consuming. If I prepare them this evening it will help me complete the order by the time Aunt's client arrives tomorrow. Remember, there's a deadline to meet.'

'OK. Point taken.' He crossed the kitchen and made an exit through the back door, closing it with a slight slam.

Carla ran to the door and snatched it open. 'Luke, wait for me—I'm coming with you.'

Fleur finished stacking plates into the dishwasher. She wiped the bench, then went to the workroom where she placed a selection of flowers in a basket. A roll of tape, a bundle of fine wire and the clippers were put into a flat box, then she returned to the living-room where she settled down on the settee to begin work.

Jessica sat in a chair beside the fire. 'You're a good girl,' was all she said, her eyes returning to the television screen.

Fleur worked in silence, placing each completed flower in

the flat box at her feet, and while her finger movements were automatic, her mind was upon Carla and Luke. He had not asked the blonde to go with him, so what sort of a reception would Carla receive when she caught up with his long strides? Nor had he taken a torch, so would he take her hand to guide her through the darkness?

The tardiness of their return was something else that Fleur noticed, and as the minutes ticked away she found herself watching the door until eventually she became plagued by the suspicion that she had been a fool to have put the wiring of stems before a walk in the moonlight with Luke. And suppose he had kissed her again? So what? All that was necessary was a firm but polite refusal and he would soon get the message. And then a disturbing thought struck her. Did she really want to give him that message?

At last the forceful closing of the back door echoed to reach her ears. It indicated their return, but as they entered the living-room she sensed that the walk had not been a success. Luke's expression hinted at suppressed irritation, while Carla's cheeks were flushed. Fleur also imagined she could see a trace of tears, therefore she was not surprised when Carla announced her intention of going upstairs.

'Goodnight, Jess,' she said in a voice that held a slight quaver. 'I'm going to bed to write letters.' Then, ignoring Luke and Fleur, she left the room abruptly.

Jessica sent a puzzled glance towards Luke. 'Is there something wrong? I hope you haven't upset Carla. I don't know how I'd cope with this place without her.'

'So you persistently remind me,' he retorted with a slight shrug. 'Would you like to see the news?' He removed the wrapper from the neatly rolled paper and handed it to Jessica.

She waved it aside. 'No, thank you. I've already seen enough of the news on television. Nothing but doom and gloom with countries at each other's throats. I'd prefer to read something more pleasant like a nice romance, so I'm going to bed to finish my book by Dorothy Eden. I always enjoy her books.' She stood up stiffly and walked slowly towards the door where she paused to look from Fleur to Luke. 'Goodnight. Don't work too long, Fleur, you've had a big day.'

Fleur smiled at her. 'Goodnight. I'll just wire the flowers I have here.' She bent over the work thoughtfully, instinct telling that her aunt might be going to bed, but on the way she would make an effort to discover what had upset Carla. And the answer to that, she felt sure, lay with Luke Riddell. Would Carla tell Jessica of the scene she had witnessed in the workroom?

She did not have to look up to know that Luke continued to stand before the fireplace, and as she kept her head bent over the task of pushing fine wires through the straw-like flower heads she became fully aware of the intangible aura of male vitality which seemed to exude from every fibre of his body.

She heard him open the paper, and, apart from a crackle of burning logs in the fireplace, the silence of the room was broken only by the rustle of turning pages. Without raising her eyes, she knew when the paper was folded and dropped on a chair, and her breath quickened as he moved to sit beside her on the settee.

He said nothing, and the room's silence continued while he watched her slim fingers bind tape to the wired stems. Eventually, as she placed a completed flower in the flat box at her feet, he said, 'I can see why Jess is having difficulty. I'm afraid the day is approaching when her arthritic fingers will cause her to give up.'

'That'll be sad. It's been an important occupation for her.'

His eyes on her face, he asked, 'Is this how you spend your evenings at home?'

'Certainly not.' She felt nettled by the question.

His fingers stroked her cheek as he spoke teasingly. 'Ah, then you are taken out occasionally?'

She turned to look at him, indignation flashing from her

eyes. 'That surprises you?'

'Not really.' He watched her intently, then drawled, 'Tell me about the leading contender.'

She bent over her work then said with a touch of defiance, 'Well, there's Craig Quinn.'

'Quinn? Who is he? Somebody special?' The questions were snapped abruptly.

'He's a junior partner in my father's firm.'

'Ah, a rising young lawyer. Somebody in the firm. Most suitable by the sound of him.'

'Daddy says he's an up-and-coming young man,' she said defensively. 'He says that Craig has goals ahead of him.'

'The first being marriage with the boss's daughter,' he commented drily. 'Indeed, he's obviously quite smart.'

The look she sent him was full of curiosity. 'Why does this—this situation interest you?'

He frowned as though the question puzzled him. 'I'm not sure, but there must be a reason somewhere, if only I could put my finger on it.' Then, veering away from the subject, he asked, 'The continual making of baskets doesn't become tedious?'

'Continual? There is other work to be done, you know. As for the baskets, I enjoy doing the ones that contain real gifts. They are always special orders such as a birthday present being hidden under the flowers, handkerchiefs set among the blooms, or the mother of a new baby can be given one with the blossoms arranged around small items for the little one.'

He watched her work until the last delicate stem had been wired, then, as she stood up and moved towards the hearth to brush her skirt free of floral scraps, he lifted the flat box with its careful packing of prepared flowers.

She followed him while he carried it to the workroom and placed it on the bench, then noticed the determined glint in his eyes as he turned to her and said, 'You're now ready for a breath of fresh air?'

The suggestion startled her. 'You mean——?'

'I mean a walk down the drive like the one you refused earlier. The air is quite balmy for April, and there's a full moon. It's almost—romantic.'

'I—I'm not really looking for romance,' she told him stiffly and without looking at him.

'You're not? No, of course not. At least, not with Mr Quinn waiting in the wings, ready to step on stage. In the meantime I'll take care of you on his behalf.' He removed a red and green tartan cape from a hook behind the door, and as he placed it about her shoulders he said, 'You'd better put this on. Jess uses it when going out to her storeroom on a wet or cold day.'

His fingers fastened the button beneath her chin, lingering as they touched her throat then moving gently to stroke her neck. A firm finger beneath her chin tilted her face upwards and it seemed as if his lips were about to be laid upon her.

She caught her breath, waiting for his head to lower, but although he gazed at her for a long moment he merely said, 'Let's go.'

Vaguely conscious of disappointment, she allowed herself to be led through the door at the end of the short passage and out into the night. As they walked round the corner of the house she wondered why she didn't face him with determination and tell him she had no intention of walking along that dark avenue; but instead she went meekly, making no objection when he took her arm as they drew near to the gloom of the trees where high branches stretched to meet overhead.

Yet all was not completely dark, because the full moon sent shafts of light to dapple the ground with pale patches, and as they emerged from the avenue the fields on either side were bathed in an eerie glow. Even the man beside her took on an air of mystery, causing her to feel she was walking beside a tall, dark stranger whose face had been made inscrutable by the shadows and whose thoughts she was unable to fathom because he did not break the silence that lay about them. As he had said, there was romance in the air, but she must not allow it, or the nearness of him, to go to her head.

In an effort to keep her feet on the ground she sought for normal conversation, and looking towards the property's back country she remarked lightly, 'The hills seem to be so misty and far away.'

'Yes, they're a fair distance. Rivermoon covers a thousand acres.'

'So much? You must have a large flock of sheep.'

He paused before saying casually, 'About two hundred, plus a small herd of Aberdeen Angus cattle.'

His hesitation had not been lost on her, and after a moment's thought she said, 'I'm sorry, I shouldn't have mentioned such things. It has caused you to reveal affairs that must be private.'

'Has it? I hadn't noticed. Nor can I see that it matters.'

'In this case it matters to me,' she told him quietly.

He swung her round to face him. 'What are you thinking about?'

'It matters when one knows one is thought of as being interested only in people's possessions,' she flung at him. And as his previous accusation rose to hit her with a force that hurt, the magic of the moonlit night disappeared.

'I suppose you're referring to my remarks concerning your aunt's windfall, and it seems to me that you find it impossible to free your mind of all grievances.'

'That is not true, but as you did make that statement one can only assume that the belief is still well embedded in your mind. Nor are you a man who is likely to change his mind.' The last words had caused her lip to tremble and, moving away from him, she negotiated the cattlestop, then crossed the road to stare at the river.

He was beside her in a moment, his hands on her shoulders swinging her round to face him again. His eyes, shadowed by moonlight, glared down into hers. 'You find it impossible to forgive and forget?' he demanded harshly.

'Quite impossible,' she was goaded to reply, at the same time knowing this to be a lie. Of course she could forgive and forget, but she had no intention of admitting this to him.

'In other words, you're exactly like your aunt and your mother,' he lashed out at her in a tone of disgust. 'You'll hold on to your grudge for ever and a day.'

'Definitely.' She turned away, annoyed with herself. Why on earth was she behaving in this manner, and why was she allowing him to believe these things of her? They were quite untrue, because she knew she was more like her father than her mother. Daddy was one of the mildest and most forgiving people she knew, but this was another fact she had no intention of divulging. If this accusation concerning her character was something further Luke intended to believe—well, so be it.

The lights of an approaching car revealed the angry expression on his face, and after it had swept past she turned again to stare down at the dark, gliding waters of the river. Her heart was heavy and she kept calling herself a fool, but pride forbade that she attempted to exonerate herself.

'Are you determined to quarrel with me?' he asked.

She shrugged. 'I have no wish to quarrel with anyone, but you might as well know that when I'm deeply hurt it takes more than five minutes to get it out of my system. Your accusation that I'm no more than a gold-digger is something I'm unlikely to forget. Now then, may we change the subject?'

'Gladly.' The word was snapped crisply.

She raked her mind for a topic, and as she stared at the silent waters flowing below them she said, 'Tell me about the river.'

A laugh escaped him. 'How long have I got? It would take days to give you a complete story of the river. It has a history of Maori warfare, and later came the struggles of European pioneers who battled to settle the land on either side of the water.'

'A story of loneliness and hardship, I suppose.'

'There were no roads, therefore the early settlers travelled up and down the river by canoes and later by steamships. Today a more modern vessel takes tourists on a leisurely scenic wilderness trip, and there are jet-boat tours that negotiate the narrower reaches that lie between high bushclad walls.' He paused, turning to look at her. 'Would you like to take a river trip? It could be arranged.'

She smiled as her normal good humour became restored. 'It would be pleasant, but I'm afraid I haven't the time. Tomorrow I'll do my best to finish the second half dozen baskets, and as soon as Aunt's client has approved of them I'll be on my way, speeding home.'

'You'll go so soon?'

'Of course. What else did you expect?'

'I had hoped that, for Bob's sake, you'd make an effort to discover why your aunt has her bouts of fretting.'

'Personally I suspect they're merely her normal sessions of ill-temper which have flared up ever since I can remember. Uncle Bob should be well used to them.'

Luke shook his head doubtfully. 'There's more to it than plain ill-temper, and I can only imagine it's an inner desire for reconciliation with her sister.'

'In which case she's had years to do something about it,' Fleur reminded him, conscious of a sudden impatience, and although this particular topic seemed to have reached an impasse she added wistfully, 'I wish I could do something about bringing them together. I've thought about it, but the solution escapes me.'

'You feel it's a hopeless case?'

'Would you believe that Aunt hasn't mentioned Mother's name, not even once? Sisters should not carry on in that manner.' She sighed, swept by a sudden tide of weariness as an uncontrollable yawn escaped her.

He said quickly, 'You're tired. It's time you were in bed.

We'll go back to the house at once.'

They crossed the road and made their way over the iron bars of the entrance cattlestop, then walked along the drive towards the avenue of trees. The brilliance of the full moon illuminated the surface of the metalled driveway, causing it to look like a pale ribbon stretching before them, and as the way was so clear he made no attempt to take her arm.

By the time they reached the dappled gloom of the avenue she was conscious of a feeling of anticlimax, although what she had expected from this walk in the moonlight she was unable to say. But as far as she could see it had resulted in little more than bickering, and this had been her own fault entirely.

Much of the trouble had been caused by the bubbling of her own inner resentment, but hadn't he given her cause to feel annoyed? That remark about her being like her mother and aunt—uttered in such a derisive tone—wasn't that cause for injured feelings? It was not that she objected to being told she was like her mother, but she drew the line at being told she was like Aunt Jessica.

They were half-way along the avenue, walking in what could only be termed a strained silence, when the quiet of the night was shattered by a clamour that sent Fleur leaping closer to Luke's side. The noise brought them to a standstill, causing them to gaze upward as the thrashing of branches was accompanied by wild chattering screeches that sounded as if several demons had been let loose.

The noise seemed to be directly overhead, and then a small scream escaped her as two whirling, clawing, long-tailed bundles of fur dropped from above to land on the drive almost at their feet.

She clung to Luke, then stood paralysed as the two animals sped away in different directions. 'Wh-what was that?' she gasped, her heart still pounding from fright, and hardly aware that he was now holding her closely against his chest.

'Only two male possums fighting,' he said nonchalantly. 'It wsa probably an argument over territory—this is my tree, you get out, that sort of discussion.'

She continued to lean against him, still feeling shaken. 'Only possums—but they looked so big.'

'They find plenty of food in the avenue.'

They had not moved during his explanation and the silence about them was broken only by the rustle of leaves in a slight breeze. She stirred, expecting his arms to release her, but their hold tightened about her form, causing her to look up at him wonderingly.

He was gazing down into her face, his eyes lost in the shadows as his head bent and his mouth was laid gently upon hers.

CHAPTER FIVE

THE kiss took Fleur by surprise. Her mind had been on the possums, while the shelter of Luke's arms had acted as a haven of safety. But even more surprising was the flare of excitement that raced through her veins, the leaping of her pulses that thumped like small pistons in her body's motor. Her hands went to his shoulders with the firm intention of pushing him away, but there they stayed until an irresistible urge caused them to creep up and find their way round his neck.

The action brought the sound of a satisfied murmur from him, and seemed to be the sign for his kiss to deepen. His hands moved over her back in a series of gentle circles, their pressure becoming firmer as they descended until the closeness of his body caused her to gather her wits, and to try to see through the haze of the emotions over which she seemed to have no control.

Her hands returned to his shoulders, and she broke the spell of the embrace by turning her face away while murmuring, 'Please, Luke, that's enough——'

He peered at her through the gloom. 'You're no longer afraid?'

'Of the possums? No, they've gone.'

'I meant afraid of me.'

'To be honest, I was mad with you, rather than afraid.'

'But you're not angry now?'

'I don't know. Only time will tell. When I start recalling your accusation I'll probably become infuriated all over again.'

'Perhaps I can help you to forget those remarks.' His arms

moved to draw her closer again.

'No, no more—please.' She stepped aside and out of his reach, then turned and ran towards the house.

His long strides enabled him to catch up within moments, and again she found herself being held firmly in his arms, her breasts pressed against the hardness of his chest and his lips on hers. But despite the moulding of her form against the contours of his muscular body the kiss was gentle, provocatively teasing, its effects being even more potent than that of the previous one.

At last he released her, and, staring down into her face he drawled in amused tones. 'There now, you'll be able to go home and admit to that rising young lawyer you've been kissed by somebody else. How will you cope with his rage when he jumps up and down?'

She giggled, feeling suddenly helpless.

He went on, 'If Bob's car lights had swept into the drive in time to pick up the sight of you running from me he'd have wondered what the devil was going on.'

Her chin rose a fraction. 'You'd have been able to assure him that nothing was going on, nothing at all.'

'So why run away?'

She remained silent, unable to explain that a sudden fear of her own treacherous emotions had sent her fleeing from further, and perhaps deeper, involvement with him.

'Well?' he prompted.

She used her weariness as an excuse, and as they reached the house she said, 'I'm afraid I'm too tired to think straight. Even Aunt admitted I'd had a heavy day, and tomorrow she'll expect me to be as fresh as the morning dew.'

'Then it's time you went to bed, but first you'll have a hot drink.'

'No, it doesn't matter. I mean about the drink.'

He waved her objection aside. 'It'll help you sleep. I suspect your nerves are rather jangled after possums have almost dropped on your head in the dark.'

That, and other things, she thought, watching him take milk from the fridge and a packet of Milo from a cupboard. And when he placed the hot drink on the kitchen table she said, 'Thank you, you're very kind and thoughtful.'

He grinned. 'Am I? I seem to have been fairly successful in upsetting you.'

She veered away from the subject of herself by saying, 'And Carla. You upset her this evening. When she came in I saw traces of tears.'

He was startled. 'You did? I noticed she became quite snappy with me, and then she turned on a fit of the sulks. Heaven alone knows why.'

Fleur sipped the hot chocolate-flavoured Milo. 'You must have said something that really annoyed her.'

His dark brows drew together. 'As far as I can recall, the chat between us was of no importance whatever. At the road entrance we were delayed by having to search for the paper which had been thrown into the paddock instead of on the driveway, and on the way back to the house she told me about a man she knows.'

Fleur's interest quickened. 'Oh? Somebody special?'

His shoulders lifted slightly. 'He's just some chap who has asked her to go out with him. She wondered if I'd mind.'

'And would you?'

'Of course not. Why the devil should I mind? And that is exactly what I asked her. I pointed out that she should have a string of men asking her out, and if she didn't have a few admirers now, when would she expect to have them? That's when she became sulky.'

'Perhaps she thought you were being cruel.'

'It's possible. Actually I was being kind. I told her to invite the man to dinner if she felt so inclined.'

'And that didn't make her feel more cheerful?'

'Not one little scrap. She hissed something about getting the message.' He paused to stare into his cup then said briskly, 'As for being cruel, there are times when one has to be cruel to be kind.

She sent him a level glance. 'Ah, so you are not as naïve as you would have me suppose.'

'What do you mean?' he hedged.

'I mean about Carla, of course. You know perfectly well that she's—fond of you.'

'And I'm fond of Carla. I know her very well, to say nothing of the direction in which her mind has been working for the last couple of years. But fond does not spell the word "love". Nor do I intend to marry her because she cooks well, runs this house with aplomb and because Jess imagines she can't live without her. I shall marry Carla only when *I* can't live without her.'

'By that time she could be married to somebody else,' Fleur put in slyly.

His gaze became concentrated, and it was as though he appeared to be pondering this possibility, but all he said was, 'It's high time you were in bed.

Later, as she lay wide-eyed in the darkness, she tried to relive the events of the day, but everything seemed to converge into one hazy blur. Everything, that was, except his face, which hovered above hers until even that, too, faded as she fell asleep.

The sun was shining when Fleur woke next morning. She sprang out of bed and experienced the pleasure of using the guest-room's en suite bathroom, and as she stood beneath the shower's flow of soothing hot water she considered the remaining gift baskets that still waited to be filled. How could she make them different from the others?

A short time later she was still pondering this question while gazing at the view from the bedroom window. The tall Lombardy poplars, clothed in the bright yellow of autumn, threw long dark shadows across the lush, flat pastureland lying between the hills and the River Road. Across the road, bordered by sun-touched willows, the deep river flowed in dark silence, and suddenly the scene gave her the idea she sought. Contrast was the answer. She must aim at light against dark, and although she realised she could work only with the materials available, she was filled with enthusiasm as she hurried downstairs.

When she entered the kitchen she discovered Carla to be the only one there. The table was being cleared of dishes, food was being put away and the blonde girl threw her a look of resentment.

'You're late. You've been holding me up,' Carla reprimanded her.

'I'm sorry, I slept later than I intended.'

'I'll bet you stayed up until all hours with Luke. Go on, admit it,' she added fiercely as she began stacking plates in the dish-washer. Then, as Fleur made no reply she went on, 'The men had breakfast ages ago and Jess had hers in bed.'

Fleur's brows rose. 'In bed? She's all right?'

'Of course she's all right. She's just having one of her *off* days.' Carla's tone became abrupt. 'I presume Luke told you she becomes depressed and has bouts of fretting.'

'Yes, he told me.'

'OK, so today you'll see it for yourself. Would you like an egg? Boiled, poached or fried with bacon?' Her manner indicated that this represented an extra chore she could do without.

'Boiled, thank you, but I can fix it. There's no need for you to bother about my breakfast,' Fleur assured her hastily. Moments later as the egg sat in the bubbling water and the pop-up toaster browned two slices of bread, she watched Carla put flour, butter and other ingredients into a food-processor. 'You're doing some baking?' she asked by way of breaking the silence that had settled between them.

'Scones, for when the men come in for their mid-morning

coffee-break.' Carla's tone had become surly, then continued with further resentment as she added, 'No doubt you'll be interested to know that your aunt is pleased with what you've been doing in the workroom. She sang your praises when I took her breakfast up to her.' The last words held bitterness.

Fleur ignored her tone and showed only surprise. 'Aunt sang my praises to you?'

'Not to me. It was to Luke. He happened to come in to see how she was. I've never heard her sing *my* praises to him.' Carla's intense irritation brimmed as she added, 'Naturally, it's easy to follow her trend of thought. She's got a plan in mind. She's laying you across his track, hoping he'll try to persuade you to stay longer—perhaps for ever.' Her resentment caused her voice to shake.

Fleur laughed. 'Don't tell me you imagine she's match-making.'

'Why not? It would suit her nicely to have you here on a permanent basis.' The anger simmering in Carla's mind caused a green glitter to flash from her eyes as she snapped, 'I think it's a rotten trick after all I've done for her. She knows perfectly well that I've—that I've——'

'That you've got your sights set on him?' Fleur felt compelled to say. 'Carla, I'm afraid you've got it the wrong way round. You'll get nowhere with Luke until he gets his sights on you.'

'You said something to that effect before, something about making him jealous.'

'If he actually saw you with somebody else it might have a result,' said Fleur quietly, then wondered why she was offering this advice. The conversation was rapidly becoming distasteful and she had no wish to continue with it. The question of where Luke set his sights had nothing to do with her, so why should it begin to niggle at her mind? But for some strange reason it did, causing her to eat her breakfast hastily, and then, having dealt with her few dishes, she departed for the workroom.

It was ten o'clock before her aunt came to survey her progress, and as Jessia entered the room Fleur noticed the suspicious moisture about the older woman's eyes. She sensed that distress lay only a short distance below the surface, therefore she said, 'You're all right, Aunt?'

'Yes, of course. What makes you ask such a question?'

'You look depressed and I—I just wondered.'

'Well, there are times when I have spasms of being upset, but I don't want to talk about it just now, especially when all these lovely baskets are being made for me.'

Fleur thought quickly. Would this be an appropriate moment to mention the subject of reconciliation? Would it be possible for her to do something about bringing her mother and aunt together? She took a deep breath and plunged. 'Aunt, can't you tell me what brings on these bouts of—unhappiness? Is it because of your long-standing quarrel with Mother?'

Jessica brushed the topic aside by ignoring the question as she began to examine each basket in turn. Nodding approval, she said, 'My dear, you've worked extremely well and they're quite lovely. I can see this one going to a motel or office reception desk. It's almost—dramatic,' she concluded, searching for the right word.

'It's light against dark,' Fleur explained. The complementary colours of pale yellow against purple and light red against deep green give a good effect.' She did not admit that the idea had come to her only that morning.

Jessica said lightly, 'You've definitely earned morning coffee and scones. We're having it in the kitchen.'

Fleur knew that the men had come in because she could hear their voices in the kitchen, and as she entered the room behind her aunt she was greeted by the sight of Carla gazing up into Luke's face as she handed him a mug of steaming coffee.

If Luke noticed Carla's fatuous expression he ignored it, but Fleur knew it changed to resentment when he moved to her side. However, there was nothing she could do about it.

'Work is progressing?' he asked casually. 'You can actually take five minutes to enjoy a coffee-break?'

Knowing herself to be under Carla's observation, she felt unable to look at him, therefore she stared into her mug as she said, 'Only three more to do before I've completed the dozen.'

'So you'll have completed the order before Mrs What's-her-name arrives to collect them. I must say you've worked very quickly.' He turned to Jessica. 'I presume it's the woman from that large florist's shop in town?'

Jessica nodded. 'Yes, Elaine Barker. The making of gift baskets is too time-consuming for her, and there are also times when she calls on me for extra help with wreaths.'

Bob said, 'She doesn't usually order a dozen at a time. Normally it's a half-dozen.'

Jessica snapped angrily. 'You wouldn't know what she orders. You're not even remotely interested in any of my work.'

Her words were followed by an uncomfortable silence until Bob replied with patience, 'Is that so? Who grows your immortelles, may I ask?'

'It's little enough to do for your *wife*, in between visits to your *club*,' she lashed at him bitterly and with much stress on the last word.

He sent her a bleak look as he declared in heavy tones, 'Jessica, you are a pain in the neck.' Then he drained his coffee-mug and escaped through the back door.

Jessica's face became flushed with anger. 'He has no right to speak to me in that manner,' she almost hooted.

'Then why ask for it?' Luke rasped at her, his face scowling. 'I must say your attitude towards Bob appals me.'

'And his attitude towards me leaves a lot to be desired,' she snapped back at him.

'I'm afraid you've only yourself to blame.' He frowned at her thoughtfully then added, 'However, there is one point I'd like to have clarified. You told me you were inundated with work and couldn't cope. You said you had orders for *two* dozen baskets to be completed by Thursday. I find that Fleur is set to work on one dozen, while Bob declares the order is for only half a dozen.'

'None of this is important,' Jessica told him coolly.

'I think it is. I'd be interested to learn exactly how many Mrs Barker ordered this time.'

Jessica turned away and it seemed to Fleur that she was avoiding Luke's eyes. She was silent for several moments before she said with a trace of defiance, 'I can't see why it should matter to you.'

His voice became hard. 'Can't you? It matters that you told me a lie which sent me to Palmerston North with a plea for help.' His face had become like granite while he continued. 'Then, when Fleur arrived, it took you only a short time to see that you had a pair of capable and willing hands at your disposal, so you realised it would be silly to admit that the order was for six, rather than for twelve.'

Jessica sent Luke a defiant glare. 'So what? There's no harm in having a few extra baskets on hand, especially as Fleur has made them so quickly and with such ease.'

'That's not the point,' he gritted. 'Does it not occur to you that it's a matter of honesty? Which makes me wonder how honest you've been concerning other statements you've made.'

Jessica tossed her head angrily. 'What are you talking about?'

'Well, statements concerning your ownership of the Fleurette, plus all that rubbish about having been robbed.'

Jessica glared at him. She opened her mouth to speak, but appeared to have difficulty in finding something to say.

Fleur's eyes were also on Luke, gazing at him wonderingly as she realised he now believed what she had told him concerning the situation between her mother and aunt. It also seemed that he cared enough about her to be annoyed that she should have been used unnecessarily by Jessica.

But at the moment Luke's mind was still centred upon Jessica, his jaw tight as his voice grated, 'You'd better understand that I consider you could be a whole heap easier on poor old Bob. He wasn't so very late in coming home last night, and you can't blame him for seeking the company of old cronies. Confound it, Jessica, the man deserves some pleasure out of life.'

His words sent Fleur's spirits plummeting to earth as the truth dawned. She had been naïve to imagine that Luke's wrath had been on her behalf when all the time he had been championing his uncle. In fact his anger had little or nothing to do with her. She merely happened to be sitting on the outskirts of his uncle's situation with Jessica.

The knowledge brought a sombre expression to her face, and, glancing across the room, she found Luke's eyes regarding her steadily. Was it possible for him to guess at her disappointment? She had no wish for him to do this, therefore she refilled her coffee-mug and said to Jessica, 'I'll take this back to the workroom. If I don't move smartly the dozen baskets will not be completed before your client arrives.' As she left the room she could almost feel Luke's eyes following her to the door, but she did not turn to look at him.

When she reached the workroom she stood still, sipping her coffee thoughtfully and realising she might have guessed that Aunt Jessica would endeavour to wring every ounce from her. It was like the old days when, even as a child, she knew that extra work was being piled upon her mother's shoulders. So what was different about Aunt Jess? Nothing. Absolutely nothing at all.

However, the memories did not alter her desire to see her mother and aunt chattering happily over a mutual interest, although it seemed as if only a miracle could bring them together. She sighed, finished her coffee, then began to consider the three remaining baskets.

Each formed a low boat-shaped container which would take a wider type of arrangement, and she knew that care must be taken to avoid flatness of form and composition. She moved to consider the various bunches of dried flowers hanging from the rack, and as she did so she heard the door behind her close gently. Aunt had come to be specially nice to her, she thought, but when she turned it was to face Luke.

He watched her choose flowers from the rack before he spoke in a gruff voice that was almost apologetic. 'I appear to have brought you here on false pretences. I believe your aunt could have managed the six baskets.'

'Oh, well, it's been an interesting experience,' she admitted. Without it she would not have felt the touch of his lips on hers, she thought whimsically, then warned herself that her mind must not be allowed to wander in that direction. Nevertheless she added, 'Didn't you say it was Carla who thought of asking Mother to come?'

'Yes, but no doubt she was firing Jess's bullets. None of us expected you to arrive instead.'

'I'm sorry, I'll be out of your sight within a short time.' Her fingers were unsteady as she placed a stem in the Oasis foam.

He moved closer to view the array of completed baskets, turning each one to examine the backs as well as the fronts. 'I suspect you feel she's put it across you—I mean by telling you she needed a dozen instead of only six.'

Fleur shrugged. 'It doesn't matter. The extras will help cope with her backlog of orders, that's if she has one, of course. To be honest I'd be interested to see her order book, except that I wouldn't dream of prying into it.'

'Anyone else would have examined it by now. It's probably right under your nose in one of these workbench drawers.'

'I am not just anybody else,' she retorted with dignity.

'No, so I've noticed.' He pulled open a drawer. 'You see, there it is. At least it would have revealed the extent of this particular order.'

She snatched the book from him and slammed it back in the drawer. 'I'll look at it when—and if—Aunt shows it to me.' Her cheeks became flushed with anger. 'Really, Luke, I'm not as interested in Aunt's monetary affairs as you seem to imagine, and as you've already indicated.'

He laughed. 'For Pete's sake get down from that high horse.' He moved closer to her, and even as he was about to take her in his arms a knock sounded on the closed door. It startled Fleur, causing her to spring away from him, and as she turned towards the bench Luke opened the door.

Carla stood in the passageway. A green light of suspicion flashed into her eyes, which narrowed slightly while resting upon Fleur's flushed cheeks. 'I'm looking for Bob,' she said. 'I thought he might be in here. There was a ring on the phone for him.'

Jessica came into the passageway. She had been in the kitchen and had heard Carla's words. 'Who is ringing Bob?' she demanded in a faintly belligerent tone.

'I don't know,' Carla admitted nervously.

'Why didn't you take a message for him?'

'I did. The person left a number for him to ring. I think it was somebody from his club.'

'Hmm, *that club*, indeed.' Jessica snorted.

Luke said hastily, 'I'll give him the message. He's not far away. He left the room to make an exit through the door at the end of the passage, his departure almost taking the form of an escape.

Jessica then turned upon Carla. 'Have you forgotten the orders I gave you?' she demanded with barely concealed irritation.

Carla turned red. 'I—no—yes—what do you mean?'

'Haven't I told you that when anyone rings for Bob and he's not close at hand you are to call *me*?'

'Yes—yes, you did say something about it,' Carla quavered.

'Then kindly remember it in future,' Jessica snapped,

throwing the remark over her shoulder as she made her way back to the kitchen.

Fleur was puzzled by the extent of her aunt's anger over something which appeared to be little more than a trifle. Surely Jessica's possessiveness hadn't reached the stage of objecting to Bob receiving a phone call? If so, the situation was ridiculous, but before she could give it any depth of thought she found Carla at her side.

The blonde girl glared at Fleur as she hissed, 'Why was the door closed?'

Fleur looked at her blankly. 'Which door do you mean?'

'This door, of course,' Carla snapped impatiently. 'You know perfectly well I had to knock when I came.'

'Oh, *that* door.' Fleur went on with her work as she added, 'You'd better ask Luke. It was he who closed it.'

Carla's lips became a thin line. 'I'll bet he was kissing you when I came. *Did he kiss you*? Tell me *at once*.'

Fleur giggled. 'Why don't you ask him?'

Carla's questions were interfering with her powers of concentration, while the mere thought of Luke's kisses were enough to make her breath quicken. A hasty glance at her watch warned that time was moving rapidly towards midday, therefore she turned to Carla and said as politely as possible, 'I'm afraid you're hindering me, Carla. I must finish these last baskets before Mrs Barker arrives.'

'It didn't matter about *him* hindering you,' Carla sneered. 'And now I know why *you* came here instead of your mother. 'You're out to catch him,' she accused with undisguised venom.

Fleur straightened her back , her eyes flashing blue sparks as she turned to face Carla. 'If you don't get out of this room immediately I'll yell loudly enough to bring Aunt at the double.'

Bob spoke from behind them. 'Why would you yell?' he asked, his sharp glances moving from one to the other.

'Carla will be only too pleased to explain the situation,' Fleur told him. 'And perhaps she'll also tell you that you had a phone call—from the club, she thinks.'

Bob looked at Carla reproachfully. 'You had only to look out of the kitchen window to see me in the vegetable garden.'

'I thought you were further afield.' Carla's excuse reached Fleur's ears as they left the room.

It caused her to smile inwardly. Carla had known exactly where to find Bob, she realised, but to search for him had offered her the excuse to look in the workroom where she suspected Luke to be having a discussion with Fleur. Poor Carla, she thought with compassion. Couldn't she see that if Luke loved her she'd have known about it ages ago? However, the urgency of the three remaining gift baskets did not allow her to dwell on Carla's problem, and she put her mind to the task in hand, choosing or discarding the everlasting blooms, and placing them carefully as she worked.

Later she knew that Carla came to the door to mumble something about lunch being ready, and she heard the trolley leave the kitchen with a faint rattle of dishes. But she was determined to have the final bow attached and the last curling trail of ribbon in place before sitting down to her meal in the living-room.

At last, with the task finished, she arranged the dozen baskets in an order that showed each one to advantage, then stood back to survey the colourful display. It pleased her, and she could only hope it would satisfy Mrs Barker.

Jessica came into the room. 'My dear, you really must come and have your lunch. We've almost finished our meal and Bob and Luke are accusing me of slave-driving——' The words died on her lips as she stared at the array of baskets.

Fleur sent her aunt an anxious glance. 'I'm coming now. I've just finished. What do you think of the last half-dozen?'

There was a long silence while Jessica examined the most recently completed baskets. 'They're—quite nice,' she admitted without any sign of enthusiasm.

Fleur had not expected an overflow of appreciation from Jessica, but the complete lack of it was like a bucket of icy water. She also realised that her aunt's earlier praise had been given when she had been anxious to have the order completed, but that had now been accomplished. She bit her lip but said nothing to reveal her intense disappointment, and while her eyes scrutinised the baskets in an effort to find room for improvement, Luke's voice spoke from the doorway.

'What's got into you, Jessica? *Quite nice*? Surely that's an understatement? Personally I consider them to be quite beautiful. Are you afraid to give Fleur the praise she deserves?'

Jessica's brown eyes flashed resentment. 'They're not actually sold yet,' she reminded him tartly. 'Elaine Barker will notice they're different from the ones she usually gets from me. She might not even take the six she ordered, and I'm warning you, she's very fussy—she's *very* set in her likes and dislikes.'

Her words sent another bucket of ice over Fleur, but again she bit her lip and said nothing because at that moment a ring from the front doorbell pealed through the house.

Jessica was startled. She sent a hasty glance at her watch, then said, 'That'll be Elaine Barker. She's earlier than I expected. My dear, thank goodness you've finished them,' she exclaimed to Fleur as she hastened from the workroom.

Fleur took a deep breath. 'I'm about to learn the worst,' she said to Luke, making an effort to affect a light tone. At the same time she found herself wishing he would leave before her aunt returned with Mrs Barker who was sure to be critical.

However, this was a vain hope because a grin spread over his face as he continued to lean nonchalantly in the doorway. 'Elaine Barker's assessment of your work is something I'm curious to see,' he said.

Fleur's expression became pathetic, her eyes betraying an inner apprehension as she said, 'Perhaps she won't like them. I had hoped to please Aunt Jess, but although she was kind about them at first it seemed as if——'

'Does it not occur to you that she could be a trifle jealous?'

A faint smile touched her lips. 'I recall she used to become jealous of Mother—but never of me.'

'You were a child during those days. Now you're a woman—and a most attractive one, I might add.' His eyes left her face to linger upon the rounded mounds of breasts beneath her blue jersey.

His speculative survey caused her to recall the feel of his arms about her body, but before a flush could stain her cheeks his eyes again held her as he spoke in a low voice.

'Do you realise that you look like your mother?'

'Yes, I suppose I do.'

'Therefore it's possible your aunt feels she's dealing with your mother all over again. History is repeating itself and her emotions of those earlier years are again asserting themselves. Can't you see it for yourself?'

'Oh, yes, I can see it, all right.'

Voices coming into the passageway made further conversation impossible, and the next instant Jessica ushered a woman into the room. The latter's severe grey and white outfit gave her a businesslike appearance, and, ignoring Luke and Fleur, she paused in the doorway to gaze at the display. 'My goodness, you have been busy,' she exclaimed to Jessica.

Jessica made introductions. 'This is my niece, Fleurette Fleming from Palmerston North, and you've already met Luke.'

'Yes, we've met.' Elaine Barker's eyes kindled with frank interest as they rested upon his handsome features, then she turned towards Fleur. 'Fleurette? You have an unusual name. I believe your aunt told me she once owned a shop known as the Fleurette. Could she have named it after you?'

Fleur controlled her irritation. 'It was in partnership with my mother,' she explained sweetly.

Elaine Barker's brows rose. 'Oh? Really? I understood that——'

Jessica cut in sharply. 'Well, here are the baskets.'

There was silence while Elaine Barker turned again to the baskets, moving closer to peer into their depths and moving each one to view it from different angles. At least she spoke to Jessica. 'They're beautiful. You have really surpassed yourself.'

'Thank you,' Jessica muttered.

'And they're so different from your usual baskets,' Elaine exclaimed, her voice betraying surprise. 'You've changed your style.

'Yes, I suppose they are a little different,' Jessica admitted with a hint of reluctance.

Luke spoke casually. 'Do you approve of the change?'

Elaine flashed a smile at him. 'Oh, yes, very much. Imagination had been used with this lot.'

'Then please take your choice,' Jessica urged stiffly, as if anxious to get the deal over and finished with.

Elaine moved quickly to select six baskets, then, pausing to consider the remaining half-dozen she said, 'I'll take them all. Please tell me how much I owe you.'

There was a mumbled discussion between the two women, and while a cheque for the amount was being written Jessica turned to Fleur with a gleam of satisfaction in her eyes. 'We'll help Mrs Barker carry them out to her car, dear. She has it beautifully set up for transporting floral arrangements.'

Luke stepped forward to help in moving the baskets to the waiting vehicle, and as it was driven away he turned to Jessica with a hard expression about his mouth. 'I must say I'm disappointed in you, Jess, and really quite surprised. One has to actually observe such things to believe them.'

The coldness of his words caused her jaw to sag slightly. 'What do you mean?'

'I waited, and I waited, but not one word did I hear.'

She became impatient. 'What are you talking about?'

His voice remained icy. 'I listened most attentively, hoping to hear you give Fleur the credit due to her. But did she get it? No. You allowed Elaine Barker to think *you* had made those baskets. It was really blatantly dishonest.'

A flush tinged Jessica's cheeks. 'Don't be silly, the order was given to *me*,' she hedged in an effort to vindicate herself.

'That's not the point,' he gritted.

'Fleur didn't mind in the least,' Jessica assured him airily. 'She's a dear, sweet girl, as you yourself should be able to see. Now let's go back to the lunch table. I must have another cup of tea!'

Fleur followed her, revelling in the fact that Luke had again spoken on her behalf. She had noticed the lack of acknowledgement concerning her efforts, but as it was what she had learnt to expect from Aunt Jessica she had simply ignored the situation.

But when they reached the living-room a glance at Luke's face indicated he had not quite finished with Aunt Jessica. A bleak expression had settled upon his handsome features, the lines about his mouth had tightened and his lids were narrowed as he regarded the older woman.

Nor had his voice lost its cold ring as he said, 'Jessica, there are a few points I'd like to have clarified, a few facts I'd be interested to learn. And I'd be grateful for the truth.'

CHAPTER SIX

LUKE'S words brought a silence to the room.

Bob frowned as questions leapt into his eyes. 'Has there been trouble? I trust everything was OK with Mrs Barker's order.'

'Oh, yes, she was quite happy with the baskets,' replied Jessica.

'So the order was for how many?' he pursued teasingly.

'She took them all,' said Jess without answering his question. 'But at the moment the subject of Elaine Barker and her order is closed.'

'Not quite,' said Luke crisply. 'I noticed that you had given her the impression you owned the Fleurette, which is something you had also assured me.'

Carla paused in the act of filling Jess's cup with tea. 'Of course she owned the Fleurette. Jess has often told me about her flower shop in Palmerston North.'

Jessica slid hasty glances at Bob and Fleur. 'I see no point in this discussion, and I'm feeling very tired.' She gulped the tea.

Luke rasped at her, 'Did you or did you not own the Fleurette florist's shop?'

'Why one arth should such a detail interest you?' Jessica prevaricated, her mouth becoming a tight line.

'Because I'm beginning to doubt many of the stories you've told me, and I'd like to know the truth of the situation.'

Jessica glared at him. 'I was the driving-force behind it,' she declared, throwing up a defence of haughty defiance.

'Until you got it over its head in debt,' put in Bob mildly. 'If Joyce's husband hadn't found the money the place would have closed its doors years ago.'

Jessica took further defence behind an attitude of pathos. 'Why are you men attacking me?' she quavered, picking up the teapot which she found to be now almost empty. 'Oh, dear, there's no tea left. Carla dear, would you make a fresh pot for me?'

'Of course.' Carla took the teapot and left the room.

Luke's voice became sardonic as he spoke to Jessica. 'Fresh tea, for yourself, but the small matter of Fleur's lunch seems to have slipped your notice. So far she's had nothing, and the remains of that cheese soufflé is as flat as the floor.'

Fleur interrupted him. 'Please don't worry about me. I'll toast a sandwich with tomato and cheese, and I'll have a cup of the fresh tea Carla's making. To be honest I'm not hungry.'

This was true because her mind was filled with mixed thoughts that darted between Luke and her aunt, and once more a glow of pleasure lifted her spirits as she recalled his indignation on her behalf. She also realised that he had doubted her previous statements concerning her aunt's behaviour towards her mother, and she felt sure he was now looking at Jessica with clearer vision.

The toasted sandwiches took only a short time to prepare, and by the time Fleur sat down to eat them her aunt had bounced back into being her old dominant self. She appeared to have become more affable and there was a persuasive ring to her voice as she spoke to Fleur.

'I'm still hoping you'll give me a lot more help, dear,' she said.

Fleur's brows rose. 'Oh? But I completed that particular order.'

'My dear, it's a matter of building up a backlog of baskets. Elaine Barker was so taken with them she thinks I should keep well ahead of myself by having a number on hand. She's sure to need more.'

Luke spoke drily. 'So how will you manage that phenomenon?'

'What do you mean?' Jessica's voice became aggressive.

'I'm asking how you intend to produce the same work when Fleur isn't here,' he explained with infinite patience.

'But Fleur will be here. She's promised to stay for ages.'

The blatant lie left Fleur speechless.

Luke rasped at Jessica, 'Is this true, or are you brainwashing yourself into believing it's a fact?' Then, as Jessica merely glared at him in angry silence, he turned to Fleur for confirmation.

She shook her head. 'I haven't promised anything.

Jessica reached out to clasp her hand. 'My dear, I want you to do so. I want you to promise you'll stay and help me. Just look at my hands, they're so painful, you can see that I need you. Fleur, I'll make it worth your while if you stay.'

The words were followed by a tense silence as Fleur became aware that all faces were turned towards her, each wearing a different expression. Jessica's held pleading anxiety, which was something quite unusual for her. Bob's raised brows indicated a mild curiosity concerning her decision, while the coldness on Carla's face spoke of thinly veiled antagonism.

As for Luke, it was the momentary flash of contempt in his eyes that caused a chill to creep through her veins. Was his derision directed at her aunt or at her? It was difficult to be sure about this, although it was more likely to be towards her, because if she accepted, here was proof of his earlier accusation, confirming his suspicions that she had come only for what she could get.

Carla was the first to break the silence, her voice petulant as she said, 'I suppose this is a family matter to be discussed in private. I'll clear the lunch dishes unless you wish me to say, Jess?' she added hopefully. But as Jessica made no reply she stacked the dishes on the trolley and pushed it from the room.

Bob waited until Carla had closed the door between the living-room and the kitchen, then turned an amused glance upon Jessica. 'What sort of enticement are you offering, my dear?'

Fleur was appalled by his question. 'Please believe me, I'm not expecting a—a reward of any sort.' She glanced at Luke to find his expression had now become inscrutable.

Bob turned to her. 'You must be given an idea of what your aunt has in mind. I'll admit it has roused my own curiosity.'

But Fleur became adamant. 'No, I'm not interested, nor do I wish to hear talk of reward. Aunt is my mother's only sister, and it's obvious she needs help. Surely I can give a little assistance without hoping for gain.' As her words ended her thoughts ran on—and that's something for *you* to digest, Luke Riddell.

Jessica beamed with satisfaction. 'There now, I told you she was a dear sweet girl.'

Luke spoke to Jessica, his voice suddenly brisk with a business-like tone. 'Nevertheless, Fleur can't be expected to work for you without a salary of some kind.'

'It's not necessary,' Fleur cut in sharply. 'I'll look upon it as my annual good deed.'

Luke ignored her interruption. 'So, as Bob says, she should be given an idea of what you have in mind.'

Jessica took on an air of cool dignity. 'Let me remind you that Fleur is my only niece and that sooner or later I'll pass over. There'll be my estate——'

Fleur gave a cry of protest. 'Don't say that, Aunt. I don't wish to hear about dying and estates.'

'Very well, we'll say no more about it, except that I'd like you to know that the money I won has been well invested. Did you know that I won a—a most *beautiful* sum of money?'

Fleur stared at her without answering. Of course she knew. Luke had told her, hadn't he? It was the thought of money that had drawn her to Wangunui, wasn't it? Of this *he* was quite positive. It was coiled round his mind like a sleeping snake.

Jessica went on, 'My investments have done very nicely, especially with bonus issues of shares, so that when I die——'

Fleur sprang to her feet. 'Stop it, Aunt,' she exclaimed. 'I can't bear this sort of talk.'

'Well, the subject of dying reminds me of an excellent suggestion given to me my Elaine Barker.' She looked from one to the other as though expecting them to be agog with interest.

'Go on, let's have it,' said Luke through tightened lips.

'She admired the lovely golden tan of my preserved copper beech leaves, and she thought they'd make long-lasting wreaths.' Jessica turned to Fleur, her face eager. 'Of course you'll have to wire the stem of each leaf to set it in the wreath base.'

Bob put in scathingly, 'A fitting task after all this talk about dying and esates.'

Jessica ignored the remark as she explained further, 'Elaine reminded me that some people take wreaths to the cemetery on the anniversary of a death, therefore she'd like to have a few in stock. Perhaps you could make a start on them this afternoon, dear.'

'Like hell she will.' The words came like an explosion from Luke.

Jessica turned surprised eyes upon him. 'I beg your pardon? What do you mean?'

'I'm taking Fleur out this afternoon. She's been in that workroom almost from the moment of her arrival. You'll not begrudge her a little fresh air, I hope? Or do you intend to constantly crack the whip?' His eyes glittered with suppressed anger.

'No, no, of course not.' Jessica looked from Luke to Fleur, a gleam of new interest springing into her eyes.

Fleur was amazed, not only by his sudden attack on her aunt, but also by the fact that he intended taking her out. 'Where are we going?' she ventured to ask.

'To a winery across the river,' he told her. 'We're rather low on table wine and sherry.'

'Is that all?' Bob asked.

Luke frowned. 'What do you mean?'

'Well, it's not very far away. Why not give her a decent outing by taking her to see the oyster bluffs or the beach?'

'You don't have to take me anywhere,' Fleur flashed at Luke, sensing he was merely performing a duty.

'You could show her the view from the tower,' said Bob.

'Yes, that's an idea. I haven't been up it for ages.' Luke turned to Fleur. 'We'll leave in half an hour.'

Her eyes widened slightly. 'I don't want to go up into a tower. I don't like heights.'

'This one won't worry you. Wear shoes for walking on the beach. A breath of sea air will do us both good.' Then, as she continued to hesitate, he said heavily, 'Of course, if you've no wish to come with me and would rather get stuck in to copper beech leaves for wreaths I'll quite understand——'

She pulled herself together. 'Definitely not. Please—I'd like to come with you. I'll get changed at once.' She made an effort to sound normal and to hide the sudden excitement brought on by the knowledge that she was going out with him.

Half an hour later the feeling of animation had slid into a

state of unreality as she sat beside him while the car sped along the River Road towards the city. She had changed into a pleated sand-coloured skirt and matching jacket and a figured peach blouse, and as they drove over the bridge to cross the river her mind lapsed into a state of being as dreamy as the waters flowing beneath them.

Traffic was more intense across the bridge, and as they passed a row of riverside motels it dawed upon her that Luke had had little to say since leaving home. Instead of chatting he had sat with his hands resting lightly on the steering-wheel, and she now took furtive peeps at his profile of straight nose and firm chin, then wondered what sort of thoughts could be causing the frown that darkened his brow.

At last she said, 'Something is worrying you, Luke. You've scarcely spoken since we left Rivermoon.'

'Boorish, am I?'

'I didn't say that, but you do appear to have something on your mind.'

'Would it surprise you to know that you're part of it?'

'Not at all. Your frown hints that your thoughts are un-pleasant—and I can still sense your underlying antagonism towards me.' Fleur added bleakly, turning to stare unseeingly at trees lining the riverbank. Somehow the joy of being taken out was slipping away.

'Antagonism? I've never felt actual antagonism towards you,' he said soberly. 'Haven't there been moments when you've sensed that my feelings have been—just the opposite?'

'Well, maybe——'

'However, I'll admit there have been times when I've felt unsettled about you.' He paused to turn and grin at her. 'But you'll be glad to know I've got over that.'

'*Glad*? Why should I be glad?' she bristled. Good grief, did all handsome men consider themselves to be God's gift to women? And suddenly she knew that her mind would be

easier if this particular face did not fill her with such satisfaction.

He shot a glance at her. 'You're not glad?'

'Interested, perhaps,'she conceded loftily.

'Thank you, at least for that much.'

She stared straight ahead. 'Perhaps you could tell me the
reason for your—er—unsettled state of mind, although I can
understand why you were so annoyed when I arrived
instead of Mother.'

'Very well, I suppose you've a right to know. It began in
Palmerston North when you tried to explain the reason for
the split between your mother and your aunt. To be honest,
I didn't believe you.'

'Thank you for considering me to be a liar,' she snapped,
then added silently, and so you drove away without a back-
ward glance.

He went on, 'When I reached home I grabbed Bob by the
ear and tackled him about it. Eventually he gave me the
whole story and since then I've watched history repeating
itself in Jessica's attitude towards you.'

'So despite your questions at the lunch table you knew
she hadn't owned the Fleurette.'

He laughed. 'Yes, but getting her to admit it is something
else.'

Fleur remained silent as she visualised Luke wringing the
story out of Bob. But while it cleared that aspect of the
situation, it did nothing to exonerate her from the gold-
digging tendencies he was so sure she possessed. If only he
hadn't told her about Jessica's windfall, she thought
bitterly, as a deep sigh escaped her.

He caught the sound of it. 'Something still nags at you?'

She shook her head. 'It doesn't matter now although I'm
glad you know I told you the truth about the state of affairs
at the Fleurette.' What did matter, of course, was the other
question, but pride wouldn't allow her to mention it. He

would just have to cling to his own conclusions. She sighed again as her thoughts returned to her mother and aunt. 'It's strange to see two sisters who are so different. Mother is a bright, happy person.'

'Jess is ruled by a different trend of thought,' he said. 'Bob declares she brainwashes herself into believing what she wants to believe. I think he could be correct in that diagnosis.'

'Of course he's right. Poor Aunt Jess, it's like a mental condition. From now on I'll be more thoughtful for her.'

'Does that mean you'll not rush home at once?'

'I—I don't know.' She stole a peep at him. Had there been a note of hope in his voice, or had it been her imagination?

'I was wondering about the wreaths she wants you to make. See, there's the cemetery.' He nodded towards the left where an extensive area was covered by rows of headstones.

'I'll have to think about it,' she said.

'Watching your efficiency while working has made me realise how very slow and awkward Jess has become, especially when handling such items as fine wires and small ribbon bows.'

Fleur's heart was filled with sympathy for her aunt. 'It's the intricate jobs that defeat her poor arthritic fingers.'

'And so she's told herself you'll be there for ever more, or almost.'

'I feel sorry for her, but if she imagines I'll desert Mother she'll have to think again.'

'Your mother will be deserted when you marry,' he pointed out.

'Only if I marry a man who lives a distance from, Palmerston North,' She was aware that the conversation was now having an unsettling effect on her.

He sent her a sidelong glance. 'Of course, I was forgetting about Mr Quinn, he who is stepping up in the firm.'

'I shall not marry Craig Quinn,' she flared angrily.

'I'm glad to hear it,' he replied soberly.

She sent him a quick glance. 'Oh? Why should it interest you?'

'Because it sounds like a contrived arrangement.'

'Are you saying you consider there'd be no love attached to it?'

'Well, you're certainly not in love with Quinn at the moment.'

'What makes you so sure about that, Mr Know-all?'

He grinned. 'Your responses to my kiss in the gloom of the avenue, remember?'

Did she remember? She remained silent, afraid to look at him lest her eyes betrayed a glow of pleasure. But it appeared the subject was not one he wished to pursue, because he went on,

'In the meantime Jess is bribing you by making noises about her estate, although anyone waiting for her to—*pass over*—will have to be patient.'

Her pleasant memory of a moment ago evaporated, and turning upon him angrily she declared, 'If you imagine I'm doing so you're very mistaken. And I'd like to know why you're ruining this outing with these insinuations.'

'Aren't you being a little over-sensitive? It was merely what Jess herself had already mentioned.'

'I know exactly what you're getting at,' she snapped coldly. 'And what's more, you're making it quite impossible for me to stay and give her any extra help.'

'That must be because you care what I think,' he declared mildly. 'My opinion of you is all that important?'

'*No, it is not*,' she almost shouted in a fury.

He laughed. 'I think it is, so we'll drink to that.'

'What do you mean?'

'We're here, at the winery. Come in and you can sample

their sherries.'

The road had continued to follow the tree-lined bank of the river and Luke now turned off it to park at the side of a large two-storeyed timber homestead. It was fairly old by New Zealand standards, and Fleur got out of the car to gaze up at high trees which sheltered gardens and picnic areas.

Luke ushered her into a foyer and down a short flight of steps to where the wines were sold, and as they approached the counter he said, 'I want you to choose a sherry that pleases you.'

'I'm not an authority,' she protested. 'At home I seldom touch alcohol.'

'Then we'll have to learn what pleases your palate.'

The man behind the counter smiled in a pleasant manner. 'Perhaps I can offer you samples?'

She watched while tiny plastic glasses were produced and then filled from a variety of bottles. Further explanation was given as the attendant said, 'That's a dry sherry, that's medium, that's sweet and this is a cream sherry.'

Four similar glasses were placed before Luke who said, 'Thank you, these samples are certainly generous.' He then proceeded to watch Fleur with an amused glint in his eyes. 'You're finding the dry sherry too sharp?'

She hesitated, then nodded. 'I'm afraid dry sherry always reminds me of vinegar.'

The attendant placed a dish of cracker biscuits her. 'Eat a couple between samples,' he advised. 'It will eliminate the previous flavour.'

'Thank you. I'm afraid I'm not very well versed in these matters,' she admitted apologetically, then hastily nibbled a cracker before forcing herself to try the medium sherry.

Luke continued to watch her, observing the changing expressions on her face as she replaced each small plastic glass on the counter.

'I can see it's the cream sherry you like,' he said. 'You'd

better have another sample to make sure.'

She sipped it while he placed his order, and as she watched the crates of wine and sherry being carried out to the car she began to feel slightly light-headed. Or was it light-hearted? She couldn't be sure of anything apart from the fact that her former anger had vanished and that she was happy to be out in Luke's company.

When they left the winery she expected him to take the right-hand turn that would lead them back towards the city, but instead he turned left and continued to follow the road which led to the more isolated areas of back country. The road became narrow and without traffic as it reached the farmlands, but still it followed the lazy river which twisted like an endless snake, writhing through the jumble of un-dulating hills.

'Where are we going?' she asked, not really caring about their destination so long as she was with him.

'Nowhere in particular,' he admitted. 'I thought you might be interested to see the road on this side of the river. It hasn't always been here, of course, and these green hills were once covered with dense bush.'

She stared up at the steep slopes now being grazed by sheep. 'It's a lonely place,' she remarked while she sat in a haze of dreamy contentment until her eyes wandered towards an area lying between the road and the river. An exclamation escaped her as she sat up and pointed. 'Look, teasels and pampas grass.'

'What of it?'

'Please, could we gather some? They're lovely heads and just ready to be cut. Pampas grass is excellent for large dried arrangements. I'd like to take some home to Mother.'

He pulled to the side of the road, then sat staring to where the wild plants grew. 'Home to Mother,' he said quietly. 'Does that mean you won't be staying, even to do the wreaths?'

'I haven't yet decided about that.'

He turned to look at her. 'Are you sure it isn't Craig Quinn who's calling to you across the miles?'

'At least he's not suggesting I'm a gold-digger,' she flashed at him.

An easy laugh escaped him. 'I don't suppose he'd dare, considering you're the boss's daughter.' He got out of the car, shut the door with a slight slam and crossed the road to where the tall teasel plants grew, their thistle-like heads bristling with prickly bracts. 'How much would you like?' he asked, snapping open a pocket knife.

As she crossed the road to stand beside him she recalled that the boot was almost filled with wine. 'Oh, just a few pieces that can rest on the back seat. And I've changed my mind about taking it home. Aunt will be pleased to have it. She's getting low on teasel.'

'You're anxious to please her?' The question held a slight ring of mockery.

His tone made her feel as prickly as the teasel. 'Is there any reason why I should not have a little thought for her?'

'None at all,' he retorted drily, then, looking about him, 'The addition of a few good pampas-grass heads should really delight her. She might even become nice to Bob.'

'I don't believe she's snappy at him all the time,' said Fleur, feeling compelled to defend her aunt.

'You don't? But then you haven't been with us for very long.' His eyes rested on the clumps of pampas grass growing about half-way between the road and the river. 'Would those be suitable?' he asked, waving an arm in their direction.

The soft, creamy plumed tops were held aloft on slender stems, and as she watched them sway in the gentle breeze she said, 'They're really majestic, like fluffy ostrich feathers, but it's wiser to take the ones that are not fully opened.'

They made their way towards the pampas clumps, Luke examining the ground for boggy patches. He walked in front, pushing his way through the tangle of roadside growth, and while Fleur was grateful for this thoughtfulness, she was also thankful he had warned her to wear walking shoes. But that had been for the beach, she recalled. Did he intend taking her there?

When they reached the pampas grass they moved between the thick rounded clumps, searching for the most suitable plumes, and as Luke's arms reached to cut the long stems she took them from him, carrying them in a bundle across her shoulder.

They were in the midst of the clumps and hidden from view when he snapped the knife shut and slipped it into his pocket. 'Surely that's enough?' he said, turning to examine her load.

'Yes, I'm now wondering how we'll get them into the car without crushing their heads.'

'You're satisfied with them?'

'Oh, yes, thank you for getting them—Aunt will be delighted.'

'Right. Then I'll take my reward now.'

'Reward?'

The words died on her lips as he relieved her of the long stems and propped them against a clump. Turning to her again, he said seriously, 'Gratitude must not only be uttered, it must also be offered.' His voice became lower as he looked at her intently. 'I've already demonstrated my way of saying thank you. Now it's your turn.'

'You—you mean——?'

'That's right.' His hands snatched her to him, and the next instant his mouth took possession of hers.

Her sharp intake of breath almost betrayed the sudden quiver of excitement that shot through her nerves, shattering her control to atoms. For a moment her fingers clutched convulsively at his arms, but as his kiss deepened she found herself pervaded by feelings of warmth that sent her arms creeping towards his shoulders and neck. Her lips parted, her eyes closed and her senses carried her away to a distant cloud until suddenly the kiss ended and she opened her eyes to find him studying her face.

'That kiss is mere gratitude for a few sticks of pampas grass?' he asked, his voice tense with emotion.

She nodded. 'Of course. What else could it be?'

'Indeed, what else?' he murmured. 'In that case allow me to show my own appreciation, my own gratitude for the fact that you came to Rivermoon.'

'How strange, when you were so annoyed to see me arrive——' Further words were silenced as his mouth covered hers, again, and where the previous kiss had been a gentle teasing that made her heart thump to send the blood racing through her veins, this caress made no secret of the passion flaring within him.

Responding, Fleur clung to him with an ardour that was foreign to her, and which she found impossible to control. She knew that his fingers threaded themselves through her hair, pausing to fondle her ears, then outlined her jaw, and as she felt his hands slide down her back to grip her buttocks and crush her against his body she became aware of hazy thoughts filtering through her mind.

Why hadn't she the power to resist this male onslaught? Instead she was adoring it, lapping up every heart-throbbing moment of it. It's just the sherry, she told herself vaguely. She wasn't used to it. And although she had tasted only a few samples they'd added up, they'd accumulated in her blood, they'd gone to her head and made her become uninhibited. Yes, that was what it was the sherry.

When the kiss ended, her senses were reeling. Her lids fluttered open to find him staring at her in silence, her eyes smouldering to reveal the desire that clamoured to be fulfilled. His hands gripped her shoulders with a force that almost made her wince, and clutching at her sanity she quavered, 'That is gratitude because I came to Rivermoon?'

He nodded, his eyes still searching within the depths of hers. 'I suppose you could say so.'

A shaky laugh escaped her. 'You amaze me. You made no secret of your annoyance when I arrived instead of Mother.'

'I'll admit I was disappointed when I realised the two sisters would not be working in harmony. Bob told me I was being naïve to expect it. He warned that they'd never worked well together and he couldn't understand what made me imagine they'd start now.'

Curiosity forced her to ask, 'So what made you imagine that such a miracle would occur?'

'Just the fact that they are both ten years older. I presumed they'd have mellowed to the extent of letting bygones by bygones.' He paused, frowning as though deep in thought. 'I suppose my real gratitude stems from the fact that I know the truth of the situation.'

'Yes, I understand.' Her spirits were sinking rapidly.

'Previously I'd been told only what Jess felt inclined to tell and there was no reason for me to disbelieve her; but now I've heard the other side of the story.'

'I see. So the fact that I came to Rivermoon has helped to clear your mind completely, and that is why your gratitude rose to the extent of offering a—a passionate embrace.' She forced a laugh to hide her disappointment as she added lightly, 'Oh well, it'll be something to think about when I go home.'

'I hope you won't go before you've made a few wreaths for Jess.'

'No. I'll see her clear of that particular order. After that I'll be on my way.'

'She'll be disappointed to see you leave Rivermoon, and as Bob enjoys having you about the place they'll both be down in the mouth when you go home.'

And what about you? she longed to ask, waiting for him to break the silence that followed his last remark. But as she looked at the inscrutable expression on his face she doubted there would be any dejection on his part. Despite the fire burning in his kisses she realised he couldn't care less whether she was at Rivermoon or more than fifty miles away at the Fleurette.

The knowledge made her feel sad and it was then she realised she didn't want to go home. She didn't want to leave Rivermoon because it would mean the end of her association with this man who stirred her senses in a manner which left her quite bewildered. No other man had caused her inside to become a quivering jelly, nor did she wish to examine the reason for it. At least, not too closely.

Nevertheless the fear that she could be falling in love with him on such short acquaintance began to niggle at her, and, turning away from him she gazed unseeingly at the hills lining the river valley. 'Perhaps I'd be wiser to leave this evening,' she said, unconsciously uttering her thoughts aloud.

'You'll throw her offer back in her face?' Luke asked quietly.

The question startled her. 'What do you mean?'

'Have you forgotten she promised to make it worth your while?' A sardonic note had crept into his voice.

The words brought a flush of anger to her cheeks. 'I can live quite happily without a legacy from Aunt Jessica,' she retorted coldly. 'And if you imagine I'll stay because of it you're very much mistaken.'

'But you'll stay for Bob's sake? She'll give him hell if you rush off before you've done a few wreaths.'

She said nothing, again digesting the fact that despite their recent kisses, their moments of closeness, he wanted her to stay on his uncle's account rather than for her own

sake. Then she sighed, realising it was something that had
to be faced. Nor was it surprising when she recalled that his
whole project of enlisting help for Jessica had been directed
towards his uncle's peace of mind.

She knew he was watching her intently, almost as though
willing her to decide in the direction that suited his
purpose. 'OK, I'll stay for Uncle Bob's sake as well as to
help Aunt Jess,' she promised bleakly. 'Now then, can we
get this pampas grass into the car?'

How quickly things changed, she thought. A short time
ago her body had been clasped closely against him while her
spirit had floated somewhere above on cloud fifteen. But
now they were apart and her spirit was below ground level.

CHAPTER SEVEN

THEY carried the pampas grass back to the car and, as she had feared, they had difficulty in fitting it into the vehicle. Long stems had to be cut, then laid at an angle which almost blocked the view through the rear window.

An intangible barrier seemed to have arisen between them, causing the drive back to the city to be made in strained silence, and when they passed the bridge that would take them across the river she sent him an enquiring glance. 'You're not going home yet?'

'No. Have you forgotten I'm taking you for an outing? Bob's orders, if you remember,' he added with a laugh.

'Oh, yes, I had forgotten.' She sent him a side glance. 'Do you always comply with his orders?'

'Only sometimes.'

'You don't strike me as being one who is in the habit of talking orders from anybody.'

'Well, Bob's a bit different.'

She stared straight ahead then said thoughtfully, 'I think I can understand why there are times when you'll do as he says.'

He sent her a quick sidelong glance. 'You do? I doubt it. However, I'd be interested to learn your—er—considered deduction.'

She hesitated, then said, 'Isn't it because his requests are like a voice that comes from your father?'

He was silent for several long moments before he said, 'You must be psychic.'

'Not at all. But as twin brothers, they'd not only look

alike, their voices would be similar, therefore it's not
difficult to believe that you feel very close to him. You even
want me to stay for Uncle Bob's sake,' she reminded him
slyly. Then, feeling that it would be tactful to change the
subject she smiled brightly and asked, 'So where are you
taking me?'

'First to Virginia Lake,' he said. 'It's a twenty-two-acre
refuge for swans and several varieties of duck. When I was a
boy my parents took me there with a bag of bread for the
birds.'

'And after the lake?'

'They usually took me to the beach.'

'Are you showing me the places of childhood memories,
or are you following Bob's directions?'

He frowned as though puzzled. 'Would you believe, I
can't be sure about that. A little of both, I think. After the
beach we usually climbed the tower.'

She said nothing, hoping he would forget about the
tower.

He went on, 'Perhaps Bob's suggestions stirred nostalgia.
I know that feeding the ducks and running along the beach
were supposed to be special pleasures for me, but I always
suspected the tower held a special significance for my
parents.'

He turned from the road running beside the river, then
followed tree-lined side streets leading westwards towards
St John's Hill. The city fell below them as a climb took
them to where expensive homes overlooked the expanse of
water edging the highway.

Luke parked the car and they walked to where children
and adults threw scraps of bread to a feathered flotilla.
Ducks left the water and waddled towards them with
friendly expectation, and as they reached the concrete path
bordering the lake white swans stretched long necks hoping
to receive titbits of food.

'I wish I had something to give them,' Fleur exclaimed regretfully.

'I doubt that they're actually starving,' Luke laughed. 'Come, we'll walk round the lake.' He took her hand and led her along a path that followed the water's edge.

The unexpected action almost sent warm tinglings up her arm, but she clasped his fingers and made an effort to appear nonchalant as she gazed across the tree-surrounded expanse where the reflected sky-blue was occasionally broken by the yellow of autumn leaves.

They walked near weeping willows that dipped long green fronds into shadowed depths, and beneath trees that lifted leafy branches. And as they drew near to the seclusion and silence of bush and grassy glades of the lake's upper reaches she wondered if he would take her in his arms again.

But to her disappointment this did not happen, and she found herself listening while he told her about the lake. 'It's abolut eighty feet deep,' he told her. 'The early Wanganui settlers named it Virginia Water after the lake in Windsor Great Park near London.'

He had dropped her hand, she noticed, then made an effort to prevent this fact from breaking into her concentration.

'At this end there's a unique memorial,' his deep voice continued. 'It's in the form of a half-canoe which has been erected vertically to the memory of a much-loved Maori woman.'

He led her towards the lofty memorial with its plaque and decoration of Maori scrolls, and as she stared up at it her heart leapt as he took her hand again.

'Your parents used to walk along the lakeside to look at this memorial,' she mused with sudden insight.

'Yes, they did. How did you know?'

'Simply because you've brought me to see it.' They were

words she had not meant to utter, but having allowed them to slip past her lips she turned to look at him steadily.

Returning her gaze for several moments he took a step towards her as though intending to take her in his arms, but instead he stopped short as if changing his mind. He then sent a rapid glance at his watch and said, 'We'll take a run to Castlecliff.'

His altered intention had not been lost upon her, and she noticed his lengthened paces as they made their way along the opposite side of the lake. It was almost necessary to run to keep up with him, and as they passed a row of large palms she panted, 'If you're short of time there's no need to go to the beach.'

'We have the time,' he flung over his shoulder.

The drive to Castlecliff took them beyond the outer suburbs of Wanganui and within a short time Luke stopped the car in a parking-area beside the Tasman Sea. However, the sight of the sands gave Fleur a shock.

'I'd forgotten the beach would be black,' she exclaimed. 'I always think of sand as being golden or at least a light colour.'

'It's ironsand,' he explained. 'It stretches along the coast for miles. We've become used to it. Children build castles just the same as in any other sand, people walk along it without noticing its darker colour. Come, I'll prove it to you.'

They left the car and within moments were striding along the beach where the sea breezes blew Fleur's dark bobbed hair about her face. They walked in silence, and her heart leapt as he took her hand again, although quick peeps at the faraway expression in his eyes made her suspect that his thoughts were hardly with her. Instead she felt sure he was reliving other days when his parents had walked along the same stretch of beach.

Just as she was wondering how far he intended to walk

he stopped abruptly and said, 'We'll go back now. There's a place where tea is served. I'm sure you'd like a cup.'

They retraced their steps and as he led her into a small tearoom she said with quiet conviction, 'I believe your parents always came here for tea after their walk along the beach.'

The remark surprised him. 'Yes, how did you know?'

She smiled. 'It wasn't difficult to guess the trend of your thoughts. Haven't you been thinking about them ever since we reached Virginia Lake?'

He gave a shamefaced grin. 'I'm afraid I've been wallowing in nostalgia. You can blame Bob for suggesting I should bring you to these places.'

She looked into her cup as she asked casually, 'Your parents always held hands as they walked along the sands?'

A smile touched his lips. 'Always. Dad used to declare that Mother was still only a little girl who needed to be guided along life's way.'

'Such short lives, she said sadly.

'Yes.' He paused then said, 'When they climbed the steps of the tower he always took her arm.'

The *tower*. Fleur's heart quailed within her as she realised that the tower was still in his mind. 'Have we the time?' she asked nervously, having no wish to go near it, much less up it.

'Plenty of time,' he assured her easily. 'You can't possibly leave Wanganui before you've been up to the top of the tower.'

Her mouth felt suddenly dry. How could she explain that the mere thought of the tower gripped her with an intense chill? At the same time she realised that the climb would be part of his nostalgic journey into the past, and she felt incapable of causing it to become incomplete. Grit your teeth and get it over, she advised herself.

Besides, a refusal to go there would lower her in his

estimation. He would consider her to be idiotic, and while she asked herself if that really mattered, she knew that it did, very much. So there was only one thing to be done. She must go up into the tower without letting him know it would be a frightening ordeal for her, and with this resolve firmly in mind she finished her tea.

Later, as they drove through the streets towards the city bridge she had a clear view of the tower standing like a sentinel on Durie Hill across the river. She stared towards its battlement top while Luke told her its had been built in 1925 of hewn fossillised shellrock dated at over two million years old, and that it stood over a hundred feet high.

'It's a War Memorial tower,' he went on. 'Can you manage one hundred and seventy-six spiral steps? There are resting places on the way.'

He found a parking-place near the foot of the tower and she then steeled herself as they went towards the entrance. The climb began, their pace becoming slower as they ascended, and as glimpses through the wall opening showed them to be getting higher she was grateful when Luke took her arm. His touch made her flesh tingle and she could only mutter incoherently when she heard him say, 'Not much further to go now.'

At least they reached the top and stepped out to find themselves the only people on the viewpoint platform. From it a vast panoramic vista stretched over the city and its suburbs, up the river beyond to a limitless expanse which took in Mount Egmont in the Taranaki province, and Mount Ruapehu in the North Island's high plateau.

But she found herself unable to look at it. She felt cold and as if the blood had been drained from her veins. She longed to crouch against the stonework of the platform's inner wall, but instead she forced herself to remain standing on legs that shook while she stared at the floor.

Luke moved to lean on the parapet. 'It's clear enough

to see the South Island,' he said. 'That high land to the south is part of the Marlborough Sounds.'

She tried to reply but no sound came.

He turned to look at her then almost leapt to her side. 'Are you OK? You're looking very pale. For Pete's sake, you're shaking like an aspen leaf.' His arms went about her, clasping her to him.

She flung her arms about his waist, clinging with her face buried against his chest. 'I—I—it's just—it's so high——'

'You've got a phobia about heights?'

She nodded. 'I'm not madly keen on them but I—I'll be all right soon. I'll get over this fit of the jitters.'

'Why didn't you tell me?'

'Because I'm an idiot, I suppose. Besides, it would have ruined your memory trip.'

'Or was it because you couldn't trust me to understand your fear of heights?' He was still holding her close to him.

'I thought you'd be somewhat derisive,' she admitted.

'Which means you consider me to be a cold, hard type of man?'

She shook her head without moving it from his chest. 'No, I don't believe that at all. You've shown too much concern for Uncle Bob, and even for Aunt Jess, difficult as she is. I think you're kind and generous, and deep down beneath that bossy exterior you're hiding a heap of love that's waiting to be showered over someone——' She fell silent, shocked by her own inane babbling, yet knowing that what she said was the truth.

'Such attributes make me feel dizzy, especially coming from you,' he grinned.

'Oh? Why should it be so strange coming from me?'

'Because I suspect you look upon me as an arrogant, self-satisfied devil, one who snatches you up, kisses you when it suits him, and then puts you down again.'

'Well, yes, you do give that impression,' she admitted.

'Therefore you, personally, couldn't care less about any heap of love I have to offer?'

'We've known each other for only a short time,' she prevaricated, glad that her face was hidden from him.

'Love can come without warning, like a thief in the night,' he pointed out. 'However, I can see that the thought leaves you cold.'

She remained silent, not knowing what to say because a denial would be a blatant lie. She *did* care about what he felt for her, and the knowledge left her feeling shaken. But how could she admit this fact to him? It would merely be food for his ego, therefore it was pride that made her say, 'I had no idea you could see the situation so clearly.'

He gave a short laugh. 'The point is, can *you* see the situation clearly?'

'Of course I can. I know your kisses don't mean a thing, so there is no need for you to fear I'll take too much out of them.'

A firm finger beneath her chin forced her face upwards, and as he looked down at her his grey eyes held a mocking glint. 'That pert remark tells me you're feeling better. The jitters have disappeared?'

'Yes, they've gone, thank heavens. I'm definitely feeling better.' This was a fact. She was feeling warmer and she had stopped shaking.

'You're ready to leave the protection of my arms?' he asked in ironic tones. 'Or would you rather stay there?'

She knew that she would rather stay close to him, but again, how could she tell him so? At the same time she knew she must now take a grip on herself, therefore she took several deep breaths of the high, fresh air and said, 'I'm sorry for behaving like a fool. I'm even ready to look at those two mountains.' She turned to gaze at Egmont's distant cone sitting on the horizon, and then to where Ruapehu rose as a massive hump.

He pointed to where the river became narrower as it snaked northwards. 'Do you see those hills to the right of a bend in the river? There's one with a plantation of pines on top.'

'Yes, I can see it. Is it Rivermoon?'

'Yes, that's Rivermoon. It's time we were heading for home.' He moved towards the doorway.

But she stood still, transfixed while the name seemed to roll round in her mind and while savouring the nearness of its tall handsome owner whose love would eventually be showered upon someone. But not upon her, she realised, because he would never love one who lurked in his thoughts as a conniving go-getter.

He looked at her curiously while she continued to stand gazing at the distant river valley and hills. 'Don't tell me you're reluctant to leave this place,' he remarked in an amused voice.

She pulled herself together. 'I'm coming,' she said hurriedly, then made her way towards the spiral steps.

When they reached home they found Jessica to be in a surprisingly cheerful mood. She welcomed Fleur warmly, beaming at her as she said, 'It's lovely to see you come home, dear. Would you believe I've missed you?'

Fleur was taken aback by the effusive greeting. 'Really, Aunt? We haven't been absent for very long.' Was there a reason for it? she wondered.

'My dear, you seem to have been away for ages.' She paused then continued to smile as she went on, 'I've been looking out bases for wreaths. I've put them on the workroom bench and I've brought the copper beech branches in from the storeroom. They've been well preserved with glycerine.'

Luke entered the living-room in time to catch her last words. He had been moving the prickly teasels and the pampas grass from his car and he now sent Jessica a stern glare as he said, 'I trust you're not expecting Fleur to wire stems this evening, because if so you can forget it.'

Jessica took on an affronted air. 'Well, really, Luke, I think that's for Fleur to decide.'

'No doubt. But in this case I'm doing the deciding for her. She's far too pliant in your hands.'

Jessica smiled. 'I remember her mother being just like that,' she reminded with a hint of satisfaction. 'Joyce did exactly as I——'

'As you ordered,' he cut in, his voice crisp. 'Well, history is not repeating itself, whatever you may have in mind.'

Fleur looked at him in a bemused manner, secretly revelling in the way he was standing up to Jessica on her behalf. Nor did she argue against it, because she had no desire to sit wiring leaves that evening. Instead she intended to go to bed early. She longed for a solitude that would enable her to think clearly, and to sort out the emotional turmoil of her mind.

The vital question had again raised its head when they had stood at the top of the tower, and now, while one half of her mind urged her to think about it, the other half warned her to push it away. It had happened when Luke had comforted her against her fear of the height. While she had clung to him she had been hit by the knowledge that she longed to cling to him for the rest of her life.

At the same time she had told herself the emotion had been born of the security he was giving her during those moments, but, strangely, the feeling was still with her. She couldn't shake it off. And then she caught her breath as she recalled his words. Love can come like a thief in the night, he had said. Had it crept up on her?

The subject of the afternoon's outing was not mentioned again until they were sitting at dinner, and as the meal was served Fleur noticed that Jessica was still in a good mood. However, this state of buoyancy did not apply to Carla, whose mouth was set with a sulky expression, and who appeared to have little to say.

During the meal it was Bob who sent Fleur a penetrating glance as he said, 'You've had a happy afternoon? Luke took you to the places I suggested?'

Luke cut in before she could reply. 'We went to all the old haunts, but I'm afraid there were a few difficult moments.'

There was a silence as surprised eyes were turned upon Fleur. She flushed slightly, then sent a look of reproach towards Luke. 'Do you have to bring that up?' she asked, knowing that further explanation would now be necessary.

'So what were the difficult moments?' Bob enquired.

'Oh, it was just stupidity on my part,' she replied evasively.

'I took her to the top of the tower,' Luke admitted. 'I didn't know she had as strong dislike of heights.'

Carla uttered a short laugh. 'Surely that breathtaking view would be enough to override any silly fears.'

'Yes, it did after a while,' Fleur conceded without looking at Luke. 'But at first it seemed to be so *high*.'

'Do all heights worry you?' Carla persisted. 'Does this mean you've even avoided going out to your bedroom balcony?'

'I haven't had time to spend on the balcony,' Fleur pointed out. 'In any case the balcony is not really high. It's not to be compared with the tower.'

'But it's high enough to scare you,' said Carla with a sly smile. 'I'm willing to bet you haven't set foot on the balcony because you're afraid to look down,' she added with a small laugh that was meant to soften her words but held an echo of derision.

Fleur ignored the remark. Balconies did not worry her in the least, and Carla's suggestion was quite ridiculous. However, she saw no reason to explain this to the blonde

girl who could believe what she liked. Then, not wishing to
pursue the subject, she turned to Bob with a question.
'You're not going to the club this evening?'

His eyes twinkled. 'No. My dear wife's rare good humour
has encouraged me to stay home.'

'It pleases you to be sarcastic?' Jessica's voice became
cool.

'Not at all, my dear. It's just that seldom or never do I
find you exuding such satisfaction.'

Carla spoke gloomily. 'Seldom or never does she get such
a good order.'

Luke turned to Jessica. 'What is this? Has something
happened? Are Fleur and I to be kept in the dark?'

'Oh, no, of course not.' Jessica smiled.

'Especially not *Fleur*,' Carla added with barely concealed
rancour.

Fleur become conscious of a sudden apprehension. Her
aunt had something on her mind and instinct warned she
was not going to like it, therefore she waited while
conscious of a growing inner tension.

Luke became impatient. 'Well, let's have it,' he
demanded. 'Obviously it concerns Fleur.'

Jessica spoke to Fleur. 'I intended to discuss it with you
first, in *private*.'

Fleur felt bewildered. 'Really Aunt, I've no idea what all
this is about. If it concerns me, why not bring it out into the
open?'

Jessica took a deep breath. 'Very well. You'll be
interested to learn that Elaine Barker phoned a short time
before you came home. She said that six of the gift baskets
had been sold by mid-afternoon. They were bought to
brighten the offices of a commercial firm.'

'So of course she wants more?' Luke enquired drily.

'She does indeed,' Jessica smiled with a hint of triumph.
'She has given me an order for *six dozen*. Just imagine, *six*

dozen. It made me feel quite dizzy.'

'You accepted the order?' Luke asked.

'*Accepted*? Of course I did. Do you think I'm crazy enough to turn down such an order?'

'It'll sure keep you busy,' Bob remarked with a veiled glance at Fleur.

'Very busy indeed,' Luke echoed. 'But what's so secretive about it? I mean, why should it be discussed with Fleur in private?'

Jessica sent him a cold glare. 'That is not your business.'

'Let's say I'm making it my business,' he said.

There was a silence as all eyes focused upon Jessica awaiting her answer, but she merely placed her hands on the table, then uttered a sigh weary enough to melt the hardest heart. At last she said, 'Well, naturally Fleur will be here to make the baskets.'

Fleur steeled herself against the sympathy she felt growing within her. 'But I won't be here, Aunt. As soon as I've made a few wreaths for you I'll go home. I belong in the Fleurette, remember?'

'Of course you do,' Carla echoed with undisguised relief. 'And I'll bet your mother is longing for you to return.'

'Rubbish,' Jessica snapped. 'I happen to know that Joyce is able to get extra help at the drop of a hat.' Her eyes became reproachful as they rested upon Fleur. 'But my dear you promised——'

'I have not promised anything,' Fleur reminded her aunt firmly.

'More of your wishful thinking, old dear?' Bob put in softly.

'Jessica ignored the remark as she gazed imploringly at Fleur. 'Didn't I say I'd make it worth your while to stay and help me?'

The words sent a cold chill through Fleur's entire body.

She longed to look at Luke, but had no wish to see the sardonic expression that must surely be on his face, therefore she said, 'I'm not in need of any handouts, thank you, Aunt.'

Jessica leaned forward. 'My dear, I'm not talking about a trifling sum given to you at present, I'm referring to something much bigger, when I've *passed over*'.

'Utter bribery,' Bob snorted.

'So, what do you think?' Luke's voice came softly.

She caught the mocking glint in his eyes. 'I'll—I'll have to consider it,' she prevaricated.

'Please do,' Jessica pleaded. 'And don't forget, it'll be to your benefit.'

The amused glint in Luke's eyes became more pronounced than ever, annoying her to the extent of causing her to say sharply, 'If I refuse, Aunt, you'll have Luke to thank.'

'Refuse? Because of Luke? What do you mean?' Jessica sent sharp glances from one to the other.

Carla uttered a laugh that almost betrayed relief. 'I'll bet they've had a quarrel. Isn't that so?' she said, sending a teasing smile from Luke to Fleur. 'You're mad with him because he forced you to go up into the tower when you disliked heights.'

Fleur snatched at the reason which would serve to satisfy Jessica. 'It might have something to do with it,' she said, avoiding Luke's penetrating gaze. 'However, I'm sure Luke will understand *exactly* what I mean.'

'Well, I don't understand at all,' Jessica snapped, irritated. 'And what's more, I'd like to be told.' But although her eyes shot questions at both Luke and Fleur, neither saw fit to enlighten her.

Fleur stared at her plate without seeing the food. She knew she would have to make a decision because her aunt would have to be told whether or not she would extend her stay at Rivermoon. She also knew she longed to do so because it would enable her to remain near Luke, even if her continued presence seemed to confirm that she was there for nothing more than her own gain.

If she went home as soon as she had finished the few wreaths that had been requested, she doubted that she would ever see him again, and the thought was unbearable. It caused a pain somewhere near her heart, a sort of cold emptiness that filled her with desolation.

Luke spoke to Jessica. 'Have you sufficient flowers for such a large order?'

She nodded. 'Yes, there are plenty in the storeroom, and more to be found in the garden although they'll have to be picked and hung to dry. Of course I'll have to order more baskets, therefore I'll be grateful when Fleur makes up her mind.'

'And if Fleur does *not* stay?' he asked.

Jessica sighed. 'I'll just have to tell Elaine Barker the order will take a great deal longer to complete.' She looked at him pleadingly. 'Luke, dear, couldn't you persuade Fleur to stay?'

'I'm afraid it has to be her own decision,' he retorted icily.

The hard note that had crept into Luke's voice was not lost upon Fleur. It filled her with rebellion, and in that moment she made up her mind. 'I'll stay,' she declared in a clear firm tone, then she looked at Luke as though defying him to question her motive. However, the contempt she expected to see in his eyes was not there, because his face had become inscrutable.

'Oh, thank you, dear,' Jessica breathed gratefully.

'Good girl.' The remark came from Bob who leaned forward and patted her hand. 'I'm grateful that you'll help Jess,' he added.

Carla said nothing. She stood up and began to clear

dishes from the table, placing them on the trolley with more force than necessary. The expression on her face indicated she was not pleased with the situation.

Fleur said, 'There's just one matter. I'll need more clothes if I'm to stay here for a longer period. I'll have to make a trip home to collect them.'

'You'll promise to come back?' Jessica's voice held anxiety.

'I'll make sure of that,' Luke said unexpectedly. 'I'll drive her to Palmerston North and then bring her home again.'

His offer surprised Fleur, especially his last words which left her mind in a muddled state. Home again? Where was home? Somehow it seemed that it was here, at Rivermoon. But she managed to send him a steady glance as she said with dignity, 'Thank you, that's very kind, but there's no need for you to do so because I have my own transport.'

'I've said I'll drive you and I shall do so,' he declared with determination.

'He's making sure you come back,' Carla flung over her shoulder as she pushed the trolley towards the kitchen.

Fleur caught the naked jealousy in the brittle voice and wondered if it registered with the other people at the table. She was determined to avoid a quarrel with Carla, and longed to assure the blonde girl that she had nothing to fear from her.

But even as she searched for the words, Luke rose to his feet and followed Carla to the kitchen. He closed the door after him, therefore it was impossible to tell what was passing between them, and Fleur could only wonder if he had found words that would be of comfort to Carla.

Jessica stared at the closed door, then she also leaned across the table to pat Fleur's hand. 'Please don't let Carla worry you,' she implored in a low voice.

'I have no intention of doing so,' Fleur told her evenly. 'I shall get on with the job as quickly as possible, then it will be high time I went home.'

'Good girl,' Bob repeated, then he sent a questioning frown towards Jessica. 'I must say that six dozen baskets is a tall order that will take an awful lot of dried flowers. Are you sure you have sufficient for seventy-two arrangements?'

Jessica bit her lower lip. 'I—I think so,' she said, now with a hint of doubt. 'To be honest, I haven't been out to the storeroom since the last order was completed. I hope there are enough.'

'That was only this afternoon,' Bob remained her.

Fleur pushed her chair back from the table as she stood up. 'I'll check what we have in the storeroom. I'll admit I've been wondering if there are sufficient colours to give variety to such a large number of baskets.'

Jessica looked at her gratefully. 'Thank you, dear. I'm afraid I feel too weary to make the effort.'

Fleur left them to go to the storeroom, pausing on her way to collect a notebook and pen from the workroom. Her intention was to make a list of the colours and varieties which were in short supply, and with luck be able to replenish them with stock from home. Mother would not object, she assured herself.

The moon had risen and sent shadows across the yard as she opened the door to the storeroom shed. The switch beside the door flooded the small room with light, and a quick survey showed that inroads had been made into various species that were necessary to give touches of vibrant colour. She began to take notes, and the list was growing in length when Luke's voice spoke from behind her.

'What are you doing out here?'

She turned to where he stood with one broad shoulder leaning against the doorway.

'I'm making a list.' The words came casually.

'I can see that for myself.' He took it from her. 'Why

do you need a list?'

'Because we're low on a few types that help to give impact to a colour scheme. I've already used numerous orange Chinese lanterns, therefore I'll bring more from the store-room at home.'

'Your mother might not be too pleased to see her flowers going to her sister to whom she hasn't spoken for ten years.'

'You're forgetting that I have a half-share in the Fleurette, therefore I can do as I wish with my half of the flowers.'

'Personally I consider Jess unwise to have taken on the burden of such a large order,' he declared, frowning.

Fleur laughed. 'Could you see her turning it down?'

'Suppose you'd refused to do it for her?'

Her smile now became forced. 'She probably thinks I'm full of avarice, just as you do, and she was relying on it.'

He ignored the taunt. 'But suppose you *had* refused?'

'Then she'd be fumbling over it for a long, long time.'

'Whereas you'll have the job done in——' He turned raised brows towards her.

She gave a slight shrug. 'There isn't the same frantic rush that was attached to the last order, therefore if I do about four each day it will take between two and three weeks. I hope Carla won't mind too much.'

A grim line appeared round his mouth. 'Why should Carla mind?'

'Because my presence in the house annoys her. Obviously, I'm not one of her favourite people.' She took the list from him and moved away to make another entry, then a sharp breath escaped her as he came behind her, his hands slipping round her body to hold her breasts in a firm clasp.

'It might interest you to know you're one of *my* favourite people,' he murmured in her ear.

'Really? You could have fooled me.' She dropped the list

while attempting to loosen his grip but it remained steady, his fingers digging into the softly rounded mounds.

He said, 'I've had a word with Carla. I pointed out that we're grateful for your help and that her rudeness to you will not be tolerated. I think she understands.'

'I see. No doubt you held her from behind while pointing this out?'

'Indeed, no, I switched her round and held her much closer, like this,' he said, his words being followed by demonstration.

A gasp escaped her as his mouth closed warmly over hers, and as usual she found herself swept into a mindless daze while he kissed her. Her lips relaxed, parting as sensation begin to build somewhere below her stomach, and it was as she became aware of his growing passion that the temerity of his words struck her with full force.

Wrenching herself from him, her eyes widened as she glared in fury. 'You've got a colossal nerve, Luke Riddell. If you think you can come from kissing Carla in the kitchen to kissing me in the storeroom you're very much mistaken. You might have *her* on a string, but you certainly haven't got *me*.' And, slipping past him, she ran back to the house.

As she crossed the yard his voice came faintly. 'I was only joking. For Pete's sake, Fleur, come back.'

But to her the words had not been a joke. They had had sufficient impact to send her rushing upstairs to her room, where she flung herself on the bed and began to weep.

CHAPTER EIGHT

WHEN Fleur woke next morning she lay recalling the incident of the previous evening. Chiding herself, she decided she had been a fool to make that impetuous dash from the storeroom. It would tell Luke that she was jealous of Carla, and the reason for this would be easy for him to guess, especially after her response to his kisses, which must have betrayed her growing love for him.

The thought of facing him filled her with acute embarrassment, and in an effort to avoid meeting him at breakfast she took longer than usual over her shower. Her late appearance earned a glower of resentment from Carla, but she ignored it and made her way to the workroom as soon as she had finished her tea, toast and marmalade.

At ten o'clock the aroma of coffee floated through to the workroom, and then voices told her the men had arrived for their mid-morning break. However, she decided against joining them and continued to sit with her head bent over the delicate task of wiring stems.

Luke's voice interrupted her. 'Aren't you coming for coffee?'

She did not look at him. 'No, I thought I'd give it a miss and get on with the job.'

'Why?' The question came tersely.

She searched her mind for a convincing answer, but could find nothing to say.

'Why do I get the feeling you're avoiding me?' he demanded, coming closer to stare down into her face.

'I am not avoiding you,' she lied as she stood up, then she

added, 'You're right, I do need a break from this concentration.' And as she accompanied him to the living-room she lectured herself silently. I need more than a coffee-break, she decided. I need time to pull myself together, time to get my emotions under control, otherwise I'm in danger of becoming as dour and depressed as Aunt Jess, and that will put paid to any glances Luke is likely to send in my direction. So snap out of it, you idiot. Try to *smile*.

It was an effort, but she managed to present a more cheerful aspect than she was feeling, and when Bob asked her a question she was able to smile. 'When is Luke taking you to Palmerston North?' he asked with a side glance at his nephew.

'I don't know. He hasn't said,' she told him.

'It'll be Sunday afternoon,' said Luke.

'Oh, thank you.'

Bob looked at her shrewdly. 'Does that make you feel happier?

She turned to him, startled. Surely he hadn't sensed her depression? 'What do you mean, Uncle Bob? Are you suggesting I'm unhappy and that I want to go home?'

His eyes twinkled. 'I just wondered if you're missing somebody from over there. No, I don't mean your parents, I mean some young fellow who takes you out and who possibly visits during the weekends.'

She grasped at the suggestion unwittingly handed to her by Bob. 'Oh, well, yes, there is someone who calls.'

'That would be the up-and-coming Mr Quinn?' said Luke casually.

She ignored his tone. 'Yes, although it usually depends upon the weather. During the summer and autumn we play tennis,' she said without admitting that this was one of the ways in which Craig monopolised her weekends.

'You enjoy tennis?' Luke asked politely.

'To be honest I'm glad of the physical exercise, because

floral work is rather sedentary,' she explained. 'It's good to be given the opportunity to dash round the court. Craig and I belong to the same club,' she added.

Carla's interest became obvious as she said with a hint of relief, '*Craig?* I didn't realise you had a steady boyfriend. Does this mean you're almost engaged?'

The firm denial that sprang to Fleur's lips faded abruptly as recollection of the earlier advice she herself had given to Carla returned to her mind; therefore she sent the blonde an enigmatic smile and said nothing.

But Carla became persistent. 'Are you almost engaged and haven't told us?'

Fleur was not to be drawn. She shrugged the question away with a light retort, 'Who knows?' She then sent a glance towards Luke, but as he was talking to Jessica it seemed doubtful that he had heard the exchange between Carla and herself.

Carla, however, was determined to make sure. 'Did you hear that, Luke?' she asked. 'Fleur has almost admitted she's about to become engaged to this friend of hers.'

He turned to look at Fleur. 'Really? How interesting.' Then he resumed his conversation with Jessica, indicating that the information meant nothing at all. 'Why don't you and Bob come to Palmerston North with us?' he asked the older woman.

Jessica's chin rose. 'Go to my sister's house? Certainly not,' she declared coldly.

'You expected her to come here,' Bob pointed out in a mild tone.

'That was different,' Jessica snapped.

Luke spoke sharply. 'Your sister held out a hand by sending her daughter when you needed help. Why can't you return the gesture by paying a visit?'

'Why? Well—because I *can't*,' Jessica retorted stubbornly.

Luke scowled at her. 'No, of course you can't, because

you are not big enough to do so. Personally I consider your attitude to be a disgrace.' His anger grew as he lashed at her. 'Sometimes I wonder how I put up with you being in my house. If it weren't for Bob you'd be out on your ear, right smartly.'

Jessica gaped at him, her jaw sagging slightly as she became flushed with anger, then, mustering her dignity, she stood up and left the room.

Bob spoke to Luke. 'Wasn't that a bit tough on her?'

Luke grinned. 'Yes, maybe it was, but it made me feel good. I've been itching to give her a piece of my mind ever since—well, for the last week.'

'Don't you mean ever since Fleur has been here?' asked Bob slyly.

'I mean ever since I've known the truth of the situation between those two sisters,' Luke told him gruffly. He paused then repeated his former invitation. 'Well, if Jess won't come there's no reason why you shouldn't come.'

Bob shook his head. 'No, thank you. My presence would only emphasise Jessica's absence. Joyce would guess she'd refused to visit her.' Her eyes twinkled as he turned to Fleur. 'In any case I'm sure you two would rather be alone.'

His words made Fleur's cheeks feel warm. The conversation of the last several minutes had left her in a slightly dazed state, and while she was glad to know that Luke now understood the Fleurette situation, she felt depressed by his suggestion that others should accompany them to Palmerston North. Obviously, he couldn't care less whether or not they were alone, and the knowledge served only to plunge her into a deep depression.

She saw little of Luke before they left for the drive that would take them to her home in the neighbouring city, and even at the meal table his conversation was directed mainly to Bob in a discussion that concerned closing fields to conserve winter feed for the stock, or the amount of hay in the barns. It seemed almost as though he could find nothing to say to her, and she wondered if he was already regretting his decision to drive her to her home town.

Sunday dawned as a fine, clear day. The morning air held an autumn crispness, while the afternoon became mild enough to allow breezes to blow in the open window of the Volvo.

As the car sped along the highway Fleur relaxed into a state of contentment simply because she was sitting beside Luke. There were times when her eyes spent moments watching his strong lean hands as they rested upon the wheel, and there were times when she took quick, furtive peeps at his handsome profile.

Little was said until he sent her a questioning glance. 'Your mother knows you'll be home today?'

'Yes. I phoned her last night.'

'I presume she understands it's just a brief visit, and that she doesn't imagine you're returning home to stay.'

'No. I explained the situation. I told her about Aunt's large order and that you would be bringing me to collect extra clothes.' She paused, then told him with a hint of satisfaction, 'Mother even suggested I might like to take some of our dried flowers back with me.'

He made no comment and they drove for several miles in another long silence until he said, 'You appear to be very deep in thought. Is it possible you're regretting your decision to take on that large order?'

'No, I do not regret the decision to help Aunt. I know she's difficult, but she can't help her nature. I suppose.'

'Then what puts that frown on your brow? It tells me something is niggling at you.'

She sent him a fleeting smile. 'I'll get over it. I'll push it away from me.'

He stared straight ahead. 'Am I to understand it is something to do with me?'

She shrugged and remained silent.

'Come on, out with it,' he demanded, his tone hardening.

She decided to be honest. 'Well, if you must know, your underlying contempt does not make the job any easier.'

'My *contempt*? What the devil are you going on about?'

'Don't try to deny it,' she flared. 'I know darned well that you consider me to be a money-grasping person who is out for all she can get from an ageing aunt.'

'Surely your instincts have told you otherwise. Where's your womanly intuition?'

'There are times when instinct and intuition are not to be relied upon. Only a fool would put too much store on them,' she retorted bitterly as she recalled the closeness of his embrace and the ardour of his kisses, while beneath them lay suspicion of her motives. The memory angered her to such an extent her eyes misted.

'Can't you see that you've got it all wrong?' he gritted.

'No, I can't.' Then pride made her add, 'But *you* can believe that your low opinion of me is of no concern whatever. It doesn't even *move* me,' she lied, staring through the side window and blinking rapidly.

And after that emphatic remark they became wrapped in another long silence.

When they reached the flat, sprawling city of Palmerston North Fleur guided Luke to her parents' home in Fitzherbert Avenue where large old trees bordered the roadway. And as he turned into the drive the sight of a car met their eyes. 'Your parents appear to have a visitor,' he commented as he parked near it.

'It's Craig Quinn's car,' she admitted, not feeling exactly delighted by his presence.

'Really?' Luke sounded slightly bored as he got out of the car and surveyed the massed reds, golds, pinks and yellows of dahlias, marigolds and chrysanthemums. 'It's a riot of colour,' he commented.

They found Joyce and Peter Fleming relaxing on chairs set on a sheltered patio where the sun filtered through the scarlet leaves of Virginia creeper. The man who was with them was fair-haired and in his late twenties. When he stood up he proved to be of medium height, while the tennis shorts and shirt he wore indicated he had come with the game in mind.

Introductions were made, and then Peter Fleming hugged his daughter. His blue eyes regarded her with a hint of speculation as he said, 'Your mother tells me this is just a flying visit.'

'Not too brief for a game of tennis, I hope,' Craig put in firmly. 'I've booked a court for doubles at three-thirty.'

Surprise caused Fleur's eyes to widen. 'But you couldn't be sure I'd be here.'

He grinned. 'Your mother told me you were coming, so I took the risk. And of course you will come.'

'I'm sorry, I don't think I'll have the time. I need to pack a suitcase and choose flowers for dried arrangements.'

'There'll be time if you get cracking and move smartly,' he said, a gleam of determination appearing in his pale eyes.

'You're very demanding, Craig Quinn,' she retorted, irritated by the knowledge that, as usual, he expected her to jump to his request.

His grin grew wider. 'That's right. That's how one gets what one wants out of life. So how about changing into your tennis outfit?'

Luke spoke to Fleur, his voice holding an amused drawl. 'There is no need for us to rush back to Wanganui, therefore you have time for several games.'

She turned to examine his face which had taken on the inscrutability she was beginning to recognise. Was he pushing her towards Craig? Was he telling her he couldn't care less whether she was beside him or a hundred miles away?

Wordlessly, she went to her bedroom, her mind in a daze as she snatched clothes from the wardrobe and drawers. Then, as she began to think clearly, she realised that to go with Craig would give Luke the opportunity to talk to her parents and to get to know them a little—especially Mother.

Besides, Craig had booked the court for doubles, which meant that two other people would be relying on her to be there, so of course she must go. And with the decision made, she lifted her tennis dress from the wardrobe.

When she returned to the patio she carried her racquet and an eyeshade. The white dress with its short pleated skirt suited her trim figure and revealed her long, beautifully shaped legs.

The men stood up and surveyed her in silence. The sight of her brought a nod of satisfaction from her father, and while Luke's face remained expressionless, an exclamation of pleasure escaped Craig.

'Ah, sportswoman of the year,' he declared. 'Come along—darling.'

Darling. She went crimson as she glared at him. How *dared* he call her darling in front of her parents and—*and Luke?* The utter nerve of him. Then, as he moved to take her arm, she snatched it away in a fury. Nor did she have the courage to look at Luke who, she felt sure, would be highly amused.

The courts were only a few blocks away, and as they turned the first corner Craig came straight to the point. 'Does that fellow mean anything to you?''

Her simmering anger exploded. 'That is not your business, and how *dare* you call me *darling* in front of him?'

Craig sent her a crooked grin. 'Just as well to let him know how we stand and where he stands.'

'What do you mean? We don't stand anywhere. I'm

merely a convenient partner when you need one.'

He laughed. 'That's what you think—darling.'

'*Stop it*,' she shouted, her fury rising again. 'Use that word once more and I shall have been out with you for the last time.'

'Cool it,' he advised. 'Otherwise your game will suffer. We must beat this couple.'

She looked at him curiously. 'Must you always win, Craig?'

'Of course. What else would you expect? However, I have not yet reached my most important goal.' The words ended with a sidelong glance at Fleur.

She did not give him the satisfaction of asking what the goal would be, and she was still feeling disturbed when they walked on to the court. It caused her to play badly, and it was only Craig's aggressive serves and his energetic dashing after the ball to hammer it across the net that enabled them to win.

She was thankful when their time-limit on the court expired, and as they drove home she waited for comment on her poor play to come from him. But as no criticism was offered she presumed it was only satisfaction with his own performance that kept him silent.

When they reached home they found her parents and Luke still reclining in the patio chairs. An intangible aura of companionship appeared to exist between them, possibly engendered by the pewter mugs of cold beer resting on the small patio table. A mug was filled for Craig, but Fleur drank only a small shandy before excusing herself to shower and change.

Eventually she went to what had become known as the home storeroom. Once it had been a small bedroom, but lack of space at the shop had caused it to be hung with bunches of dried flowers, extra baskets and other necessities. It was also a place where Fleur could work at

home if she wished to do so, and her eyes now searched the
rolls of ribbon for colours which were lacking in her aunt's
supply.

Within a short time she had filled several cardboard
cartons with flowers, and as she did so she listened for
sounds that would indicate that Craig was about to leave.
However, it was a vain hope because when she returned to
the patio he looked nicely settled with an almost over-
flowing mug, and was obviously waiting to be invited to
remain for the evening meal. Nor had she any option but to
take the empty chair beside him.

He turned to regard her intently, his pale eyes demanding
an answer. 'How long do you intend to stay in Wanganui?'

She was startled by the abruptness of the question. 'Why
do you ask?'

'Because we'll be attending a couple of formal functions.'
The statement was made with a proprietorial air, and as
though there would be no doubt of her accompanying him.

Joyce said, 'Now isn't that nice?'

Fleur spoke quickly. 'Please don't rely on me, Craig. You
know I'm returning to Wanganui and I can't say when I'll
be home.'

Joyce cut in, 'Perhaps you could use the phone, dear. You
could ring Craig and let him know your progress with the
baskets, and then he'll know when to expect you.'

Fleur became conscious of an inner exasperation. 'No,
Mother. It would be much better for Craig to arrange to
take somebody else.'

'And you've got that lovely new lilac dress to wear,' Joyce
continued as though Fleur hadn't spoken. 'Are you taking it
to Wanganui?'

'Certainly not,' Fleur almost snapped, infuriated by her
mother's hint that perhaps Luke would be taking her out.
'Nor can I guarantee to be back in time for whatever
functions Craig has in mind.'

Craig's mouth became set in a stubborn line. 'I'm not taking anybody else,' he said. 'It's you or nobody. You know we always have fun together.'

Fleur forced a smile and said gently, 'Of course we do, but you can have fun with lots of others if you'll allow yourself to do so.' She then sent a sidelong glance towards Luke and noticed the controlled amusement hovering about his lips. The sight of it annoyed her to the extent of taking her mother's advice, therefore she gave an exaggerated sigh and said, 'Very well, Craig, I'll let you know when I'm due to come home. But you must remember I have more than seventy gift baskets to make. It's an order that will take time to complete and I do not intend it to be a rushed job.'

'You'll let me know the progress,' he said in a tone that held demand.

'Yes, I suppose so.' She tried to keep the reluctance from her voice, nor was she aware of the sardonic expression on Luke's face.

'Good girl—I know we'll be at those functions,' Craig said.

The satisfied grin that spread over his face made her feel more cross than ever. As usual he was taking too much for granted by expecting her to partner him whenever the occasion arose. When she came home this situation would be ended, she decided, or people would be linking their names on a more permanent basis, if this wasn't already happening.

Later, as the Volvo sped westwards, towards Wanganui, Fleur's instinct told her that questions were revolving in Luke's mind. She sat waiting for the first one to be directed at her, and when it came it took her by surprise.

'Did you bring the new lilac dress your mother mentioned?'

'No, it's for going out in the evening.'

'Reserved for occasions with Craig, is it?'

'Certainly not,' she snapped.

'Well, I must admit he's a personable young fellow.'

'What did you expect, a chinless wonder with big ears?'

He smiled. 'One never can tell what takes a maiden's fancy. And I think you are still—a maiden. I doubt that he's taken you to bed yet.'

She caught her breath as angry colour flooded into her face. '*Really*—you've got a nerve.'

'But I'm right, I think.'

She glared at him defiantly, her chin held a trifle higher. 'What makes you so sure?'

'Because I doubt that he's a complete fool. He can see the wisdom of *hastening slowly*.'

'You're speaking in riddles.'

'He's looking ahead towards a bright future and he's got you marked down as his bride because you'll assure him of promotion in the firm. But if he moves too quickly he's in danger of ruining his friendship with you, and that could jeopardise his relationship with your father.'

She became indignant. 'Are you saying that his attentions to me are for nothing more than his own advancement? *Thank you very much*. I'm most flattered.'

Night had fallen before they left and she now stared unseeingly at the brilliant swathe cut into the darkness by the Volvo's strong headlights. At times the windows of a homestead gleamed in the distance, but failed to register with her.

'So how do you feel about him?' Luke queried. 'I mean deep down.'

She stirred herself to answer. 'Is that any business of yours?'

'I'm making it my business.'

'Oh? Why?'

'Because I wouldn't like to see you throw yourself away on a loveless match.'

She considered her reply for several moments before she said, 'Thank you for your concern.' Then a cold note crept into her voice as she added, 'Tell me, Luke, does your mind always suspect gold-digging as a reason for people's actions?'

'What do you mean?' His tone held irritation.

'Well, you're so sure that I'm doing Aunt's baskets only for what I can get, and you think that Craig's attentions towards me are purely for what *he* can get. It's not what I'd call complimentary.'

She almost held her breath as she awaited his answer. Surely a denial must come, but when he merely continued to stare ahead the silence became strained and she felt the tightening folds of a cloak of despondency.

Leaning against the headrest, she closed her eyes as his previous words returned to her mind, words about not wishing to see her make a loveless match. Was it possible he cared for her sufficiently to worry about her future? Or was his concern just part of his natural kindness?

Yes, he was definitely a kind person, she decided, recalling his anxiety for his uncle's peace of mind. And hadn't he even sought help for Aunt Jess when she had been in a flap over last Thursday's deadline for the last order? It seemed he made excuses for people, giving them the benefit of any doubts he might have about them, except when it came to herself.

When they reached Rivermoon Luke drove the car into the back yard and stopped near the door leading into the short passage. The flowers were carried into the workroom and as he peered into the cartons he said, 'You've been very generous.'

Fleur shrugged but said nothing.

'I can only hope that Jess will show you a little gratitude.'

Astonishment flashed into her eyes. 'Well, really, coming from you, that's quite a statement.' Then despite herself more words came tumbling. 'I wish I could make you understand I'm not looking for gratitude of any sort. I shall complete the orders Aunt has on hand and then I shall say goodbye to Rivermoon—and its inmates.'

'All of them?' The question came lightly.

'Definitely, *all* of them.'

'Mr Quinn calls so loudly?'

'If he does I can't hear him,' she snapped. 'Craig means nothing to me, so you can be assured I'll never marry him.'

'I'm glad to hear it.'

'How can it possibly interest you?'

'That's something I've been asking myself,' he growled in a low voice while staring at her intently, then he swung round abruptly and left the room.

She followed him to the living-room where Jessica, Bob and Carla sat watching television. Jessica welcomed her with surprising warmth. 'I'm so glad you're back, dear. We've missed you, haven't we, Carla?

Carla ignored the question. Instead, she left her chair and moved towards Luke, smiling up into his face as she asked, 'Would you like a hot drink—coffee, chocolate or Horlicks? Let me make something for you. We had some earlier.'

Luke looked at her gravely. 'Thank you, Carla, that's very kind of you. I'm sure Fleur could do with a hot drink. She's used up energy by playing tennis with her friend Craig.'

'You mean with her *fiancé*?' Carla actually smiled as she turned to ask Fleur which of the hot drinks she would prefer.

'There's no need to trouble you,' Fleur said hastily as she followed Carla to the kitchen. 'I can make a drink of chocolate.'

'Oh, no, I'll fix both drinks,' Carla assured her. 'Now you must tell me all about this man in Palmerston North.'

Fleur felt a hypocrite. She longed to say that Craig was

not her fiancé, but if Carla was determined to cling to this wishful thinking it might lead to a better relationship between them during the remainder of her stay at Rivermoon.

The next morning Fleur began work in earnest, wiring dried copper beech leaves for the order of wreaths that must be completed before she set about the task of the baskets. And as her nimble fingers twisted and wound she listened for the sound of Luke's voice, or the tread of his steps in the passage. But when silence remained she found it necessary to shake off depression.

This was how it had been for his mother, she realised with acute perception. Before her death she had known the constant listening, the sad waiting for someone who could not arrive. But Luke *could* arrive. She would see him at meal times, and that thought alone was enough to make her fingers tremble from the inner excitement that swept through her body with more force every day.

During the week that followed there were times when Jessica sat beside her, doing as much as her fingers would allow while continually bewailing the fact that her days for doing floral work were almost at an end. 'It's time Bob and I got out of this place,' she declared during one session of complaints.

Fleur wondered if she had heard correctly. 'You mean, you're thinking of leaving Rivermoon?'

'Or course. It's time we had a place of our own. Rivermoon belongs to Luke. I haven't had my own home for ten years,' she plaintively. 'And there's another complication that will loom sooner or later.' She fell silent.

Fleur looked at her expectantly. 'Yes?'

Jessica hesitated then admitted, 'Recently I've noticed him being quite nice to Carla, nice enough to make me wonder if he's fallen in love with her at last. I've noticed them holding conversations that appeared to be rather private.'

Fleur's fingers remained still while Jessica's words sent a chill through her. 'Really?' she said in a voice that sounded flat and dull.

'Haven't you noticed them walk along the drive to collect the evening paper? Not *every* night, of course.'

'No. I'm afraid I've been too busy in the workroom.' She paused, trying to accustom her mind to the situation before she asked, 'So what is the complication?'

'Well, don't you see? If he married Carla our positions will be different. *She* will be the mistress of Rivermoon. In fact, she might want me out of the house.'

'Oh, no, I'm sure you're mistaken.' Fleur tried to comfort her aunt by sounding convincing.

Jessica sighed. 'My dear, you must realise I haven't always been very nice to Carla. I've snapped at her many times, and I know she has stayed here only because of Luke.'

Dejection settled upon Fleur's shoulders. Actually she *had* noticed a change in Luke's manner towards Carla, although it had impressed her as being sympathetic rather than affectionate. But now she began to wonder if her aunt was right. Had Luke fallen in love with Carla after all? Her mouth felt dry as she tried to push the fear from her mind, and reverting to her aunt's problem she said, 'What would you do? Where would you go?'

'I've been thinking about it for some time and I've discussed it with Bob. I've told him I want a small place near the city. He can spend as much time as he wishes at Rivermoon, but I want my own home, my own roof, you understand.'

'Yes, I see.' But all she could see was a vision of Luke holding Carla in his arms, just as he had held Fleur herself.

Had his kisses on her lips been merely to test his own feelings about Carla? The thought made her feel cold with misery. And then Jessica's next words pierced her brain.

'Of course it will be better for Bob. He'll be closer to his club.'

Fleur hid her surprise. 'You won't mind about that?'

'No. I can see I've been selfish in denying him the pleasure of his club. To be honest, I've been a mighty big fool. But if Bob buys me a nice home near the city he will have earned his evenings at the club. There will be no more complaints.'

Fleur laughed. 'A sort of compromise?'

'I suppose so. Now then, I'll go and see what Carla's doing about dinner this evening.'

As Jessica began to leave the room a thought struck Fleur. 'Will you wait to hear wedding bells before you search for a house?'

Jessica paused in the doorway. 'Indeed, no. My mind is made up. I'll begin looking quite soon.'

Her departure left Fleur with plenty to think about, and while her fingers worked automatically her mind mulled over the surprising decision made by her aunt. She could only hope that the promise of fewer complaints would be kept, and that life would be more pleasant for Uncle Bob. Did Luke know about the coming change? No doubt it would have been mentioned and discussed.

And although she longed to know if Luke considered it would be to Bob's advantage, there seemed to be little or no opportunity to broach the subject. It was strange, she thought. They were living in the same house, yet she was seeing very little of him apart from at meal times when it was impossible to hold a private conversation. Was he avoiding her? The question gave her a pang of despair.

At the same time she realised it was not her business, and if Luke wished her to know his feelings on this particular matter he would tell her of them when he saw fit to do so. Possibly it would be when he was ready to admit that he and Carla had made a commitment to each other and were about to announce their engagement.

The thought gripped her mind with an even deeper despair until she took herself in hand and decided she was being a fool. The time had not yet come when a diamond glittered on Carla's finger, and until it did she could keep hoping it would not happen.

CHAPTER NINE

DURING the next ten days Fleur's intense concentration on her work kept her emotions on an even keel, although coupled with it was an interest in her aunt's housing project.

She realised that the possessiveness in Jessica's nature was again rearing its head, causing her to speak constantly of *my* new home—never *our* new home—and Fleur doubted that she had taken Bob to see even one of the houses on the estate agent's list.

But at least the anticipation of going to see yet another home for sale appeared to be keeping her in a good mood, although Bob was heard to remark that he wondered if she would ever see one that satisfied her many demands of I *must have this*, and I *must have that*.

Strangely, the enthusiasm that filled Jessica did not reflect upon Carla, who made no secret of the fact that she did not approve of this new home venture. It was almost as though she feared for her own future, and this was revealed in the kitchen when Fleur was helping her to stack plates into the dishwasher.

'It's all your fault,' Carla snapped with undisguised fury.

Fleur was taken aback. 'My fault? You must be out of your mind.'

'Oh, no, I'm not. She's afraid you'll marry Luke, and then she'll have both you and your mother lording it over her. Needless to say that's something she can do without.'

'Carla, how ridiculous can you be?'

'I am not ridiculous, but the situation is, and I've told her so. I've assured her that Luke will never marry you, and that there's no need for all this business of finding another home.'

'Perhaps you're right, ' Fleur said quietly, noting the ring of confidence in Carla's former statement, then she added, 'But you're forgetting that her object is to possess her *own* home, she longs to have her own roof over her head.'

Carla shrugged. 'Maybe, maybe not. I doubt that she'd spend so much money unless it was really necessary, nor can I see why this hankering after her own roof should suddenly rise up and hit her.' She slammed a pan on the bench then demanded aggressively, 'So how much longer do you intend to dally over those darned gift baskets?'

Fleur forced a laugh as she made an effort to remain calm. 'Aren't you really asking *when am I going home?*'

'If you want the truth, yes, I am. The sooner the better.'

'Would it be any comfort for you to learn that Mrs Barker has already collected a quarter of them, and since then I've completed several more?'

'Only a quarter? Are you deliberately doing the job slowly?'

'Are you deliberately being insufferable?' Fleur countered. 'If you imagine I'll rush the work on these baskets because you want me out of the house you can think again. And what's more, if you don't keep a rein on your tongue I'll show you what a real go-slow policy looks like,' she told Carla furiously, then turning to leave the room she almost bumped into Luke as he entered the doorway.

He sensed her anger. 'What's all this about going slow?'

'Ask your friend,' she flung over her shoulder as she almost ran towards the front hall and up the stairs towards her bedroom. Vaguely she knew that he was behind her but she did not pause to look back.

A few strides took him to her side before the door could be closed. 'I'd rather hear it from you,' he rasped, swinging her round to face him, his mouth grim.

'Oh? Why would it interest you?'

'Because I can see you've been rubbed the wrong way. Your cheeks are flaming and those blue lights are flashing again.'

Despite her anger his words brought a smile to her lips and she took a deep breath to control her temper. 'I'm a fool to let her upset me,' she admitted. 'It's—it's just that she accused me of slow work, although I can understand her wanting me out of the house.'

He brushed the latter remark aside as he said, 'I've already had one chat with Carla. I pointed out that I'd noticed her antagonism towards you, and that I'll not tolerate open rudeness to a guest.'

'You did?' His words caused her spirits to rise.

'I also told her we had enough hostility coming from Jess.'

Fleur sprang to her aunt's defence. 'But not recently. Not since she'd decided to find a home of her own.' She paused, then looked up at him. 'Carla thinks it's an unnecessary move. I can't help wondering what you think about it.'

A pleased grin betrayed his approval. 'I think it's an excellent idea. Possessing her own home will give Jess a feeling of security. It will also get her out of my house, yet I'll still have dear old Bob here during the day.'

She looked at him expectantly, waiting for him to add that there was also the question of relations between Jessica and a new bride at Rivermoon to be considered. No doubt he realised that this could reach a state of open warfare but he remained silent on the subject.

Instead, he surprised her by saying, 'I'm glad you're one whose anger evaporates rapidly. Has anyone ever told you that you're really very sweet?'

Wordlessly, she shook her head.

He looked down into her face. 'Not even that up-and-comer Craig Quinn, between serves on the courts, perhaps?'

She giggled, shaking her head, but her mirth was curtailed as he drew her towards him. Then her heart leapt as his head bent slowly and his lips descended to meet hers.

His fingers clawed into her shoulders with the strength of iron talons before his arms slid round her body, crushing her against his chest. There was an urgency that made no secret of his longing, and as the kiss deepened with his rising passion she felt herself being swept along on a tide of emotion that caused her eyes to close and her lips to part.

As she clung to him her mind soared beyond the boundaries of common sense, floating into space where it was impossible to see through a haze of intense desire. And then the world stood still until a deep sigh that echoed a grasping at control sent his hands back towards her shoulders.

Although he stepped back from her their grip remained firm while his eyes became penetrating with their intensity. They seemed to hold smouldering coals of fire as he said huskily, 'Not now—not just yet.' Then he left her and strode through the open door to the balcony.

Shaken, she leaned against the dressing-table, his words burning into her brain. *Not now—not just yet.* They meant that the time would come that he intended to make love with her, but that now was not the right moment. And when that time came she knew she would respond with all her heart, because she now realised that she loved him. It was a truth that could no longer be denied.

But did he love her? Or did he merely wish to satisfy his male needs? Her eyes were full of questions as they turned towards the balcony door, but she was unable to see him because he was concealed by the partly closed curtains. And while she longed to follow him, to stand beside him and look up into his face, pride held her back.

But not only pride kept her rooted to the spot, because at that moment Carla spoke from the doorway into the passage. The blonde's eyes scanned the room, then took a long survey of Fleur as she said, 'I know Luke followed you upstairs. Where is he? I've looked in his room but he's not there.' Her voice had become waspish with accusation.

Fleur's heart skipped a beat at the thought of Carla having arrived a few minutes earlier. 'Yes, Luke did come upstairs,' she managed to say in a calm voice. 'Why don't you look under the bed or in the wardrobe?'

Luke came to the balcony door. 'Who wants me?' he demanded, his eyes going to Carla.

She sent him a bright smile. 'You're wanted on the phone. It's something about a jet-boat. The man spoke as though you're hiring one.' She looked at him expectantly.

'Yes, I did have that idea in mind. I'll take the call in my bedroom.'

Carla waylaid him as he crossed the room. 'Does it mean you're taking us up the river? When are we going?'

He paused to speak to her. 'It means I'm taking Fleur up the river in one of the small jet-boats. I promised her a trip before she leaves Rivermoon. Now, do you mind if I answer the phone?'

Carla turned to Fleur, her eyes holding a cold glint. 'He's rewarding you for all the work on those dratted baskets. I wouldn't read too much into it,' she warned in a brittle voice.

Fleur hardly heard her, because Luke's words were swimming round in her brain to send her spirits plummeting. *Before she leaves Rivermoon*, he had said. After their last embrace how could he speak of her departure so casually? It seemed to prove that his kisses had meant nothing. In fact he had already forgotten them.

'I'd better go back to the workroom,' was all she could

find to say, and blinking rapidly at stinging tears she made her way towards the stairs.

But when she began to wire stems her fingers shook, and as she stared at the basket in hand Luke's face seemed to hover between herself and her work. There were times when she paused to gaze unseeingly into space, and as she recalled his kisses and her ardent response to them, the uninhibited way in which she had arched towards him, her face became flooded with crimson.

Now he would guess she was not only ready, but *longing* to give herself to him. Would it also tell him she loved him, and that she hated the thought of leaving Rivermoon because it would take her away from him? Within a short time she was feeling acutely embarrassed, and it was only with difficulty that she stopped work and went to lunch where she knew she would be forced to meet Luke's eyes.

But when she sat at the table she soon discovered there was little to make her feel ill at ease, because Luke's interest appeared to be centred upon Jessica's housing project, and Fleur couldn't help wondering if he had already forgotten those precious moments upstairs.

At least they had been precious to her, but had they meant anything to him? Cold fingers of doubt clutched at her mind as she listened to questions concerning the latest house insepected. It was a new unit with almost no garden to care for, and Jessica appeared to be greatly taken with it.

Nor would they have to wait any length of time for possession, although it would be necessary for wall-to-wall carpets to be laid, after which new furniture and curtains must be chosen.

Carla was shocked. 'It'll cost a fortune,' she echoed.

'I shall pay for it *myself* and then it will be *mine,*' Jessica declared with determination.

'It'll take so much of your money,' Carla pointed out.

Jessica sent her a hard look. 'So what does that matter? I

might as well spend my money on myself before I pass over.'

Bob winked at Fleur. 'Bang goes your inheritance, little girl.'

'Thank heavens for that much.' His words had swept her with a sense of relief, then she laughed as she sent a veiled glance towards Luke. 'I have never wanted it, despite the revolting opinion some people have of my expectations.' Then, feeling she had had a most satisfying last word, she stood up and added, 'If you'll excuse me I'll return to the workroom and get on with the job.'

As she left the room she noticed the blackness of Luke's frown. It seemed to indicate she could expect him to take her to task over her pointed remark, but although she listened and waited there was no sound of his tread in the passage, nor any sign of his virile form striding into the workroom. She then realised that as far as he was concerned, the matter was probably closed.

As the afternoon drew to a close she also became aware that not even the memory of their close embrace in the bedroom before lunch had been sufficient to bring him to the workroom. Her own abandoned response to his kisses was no doubt already forgotten, and the thought filled her with bitterness. She was like a piece of cake, something sweet to be picked up and nibbled at, the icing licked before being put back on the plate where she would remain until the next time she caught his fancy. The irritating picture caused her to snip viciously at several stems.

These thoughts were still with her during the following weekend when, as usual, there was little to be seen of Luke. Was he avoiding her? she wondered, watching him return to the house when lunch was almost finished. Of course not, it was merely that he had been busy on the farm. Bob was late for lunch too, wasn't he?'

But disgruntled thoughts continued to nag at her, filling

her with anger and causing her to slit ribbons with more force than necessary. 'Just you wait, Luke Riddell,' she mumbled to herself. 'The next time your arms dare to reach for me I'll slip out of the way. Oh, yes, your kisses do things to me, no mistake about that, but not one word of love do I hear.' Her voice became more audible. 'But just you watch out, Luke Riddell—the next time your face is within reach of my fist you'll get one in the eye.'

'Are you talking to me?' the voice drawled from behind her.

She gasped as she swung round to face him, her cheeks becoming pink. 'I—I didn't hear you.'

'Obviously. I seem to have interrupted a soliloquy. What's this about giving me one in the eye? I thought I heard my name mentioned.'

She tried to brush the suggestion away. 'Probably something just sounded like it. Sometimes I talk to myself—it's a sign I'm not right in the head,' she prevaricated. His unexpected appearance in the workroom had shaken her, causing her heart to turn over as she observed the shape of muscular shoulders beneath the brushed cotton shirt, and the dark crisp hairs revealed by the garment's open neck.

He sent her a penetrating look. 'Personally I consider you've been working too hard. Have you forgotten it's Saturday? Is it necessary to work all the weekend?'

'Mrs Barker will be collecting finished baskets again on Monday morning,' she explained. 'I was trying to complete a few more.'

He examined the baskets she had finished, then stood watching as she secured a block of Oasis into the one before her. 'Does she realise whose hands are behind this work? What do you think?'

Fleur shook her head. 'I doubt it.'

'Actually, I'm sure she knows. Jessica will have to face up

to the fact that you'll not be working for her for ever.'

'That's right, I'll be going home.' Despite her efforts to sound cheerful, a sad note had crept into her voice.

'Do I detect a note of regret?' The question came softly.

She sighed, then nodded. 'It's possible. I've enjoyed being at Rivermoon.'

'Have you wondered when I'll take you on that promised river trip?'

'I'd forgotten about it,' she lied.

'Or were you sure that I had forgotten about it?' he suggested slyly. 'As it happens, we're going tomorrow afternoon.'

'We are?' A smile flashed over her face then vanished as a thought struck her. 'I suppose Carla is coming with us?'

'You'd prefer us to be alone?'

She nodded, turning away from him.

'So that you can—poke me in the eye?'

'Only if you earn it for yourself,' she told him quietly.

When Fleur woke next morning she was immediately conscious of a sense of exhilaration. Today was the day, and for several moments she lay savouring a delicious anticipation. This afternoon Luke would be taking her on the promised river trip, and unless something annoying like unexpected bad weather caused an alteration of plans, she'd be alone with him for several hours.

She spent the morning in the workroom, at times glancing anxiously through the window. A stiff breeze sent clouds scudding across patches of blue sky, but there was no sign of rain. April had now turned into May, which was looked upon as the end of autumn, and as the days were becoming cooler she had discarded skirts and dresses for warmer jerseys and slacks.

They left the house as soon as lunch was finished, but before getting into the car Luke handed her a yellow windproof and rainproof jacket with leggings to match. 'Try these on,' he ordered.

She took them from him, then glanced uncertainly at Carla. 'Are they yours? Are you lending them to me?'

She gave a brittle laugh as she snapped, 'No, I am not. Can't you see they're brand new? There's even a price tag left on one of the leggings. He's bought them specially for you to wear.' Resentment bubbled as Carla's voice rose.

Fleur felt embarrassed, the colour in her cheeks deepening as she turned to Luke. 'Is that true? You really bought them for me to wear?'

He nodded. 'Of course. Put them on. Summer or winter, one wears these things on the river.'

Jessica came into the room carrying a pair of woollen gloves and a knitted cap. 'You'd be wise to wear these to help you keep warm. I knitted them years ago before my fingers became so crippled,' she added plaintively.

'Oh, thank you, and you, too, Luke—thank you so much.' She felt that words were so inadequate. Then, donning the cap and gloves she added, 'I feel dressed for the Antarctic.'

Bob, who had been a silent spectator, said, 'It can be mighty cold out on the river. The weather report says there's a depression coming across the Tasman.'

'It won't reach here today,' Luke assured Fleur as they went out to where the Volvo was parked near the back door.

Little was said as the car sped along the road towards the city, and while Fleur was conscious of her own inner excitement she also sensed that Luke was in a cheerful frame of mind. Brief glances showed a faint smile hovering about his mobile lips, and this became more pronounced as he parked the car and then led her towards a boat landing-place on the north side of the Dublin Street bridge.

It was here that a small jet-boat awaited them, and as he placed an orange-red life-jacket about her shoulders she noticed that his expression had become more serious. Something about it jerked her memory back to the day they had walked round Virginia Lake, and along the dark sands at Castlecliff.

Instinct whispered there was a connection between that particular outing and this one, and, watching his fingers attend to the fastening of the life-jacket, the answer darted into her mind. It was nostalgia. Nor was she able to resist the question, 'This boat trip holds memories for you?'

He nodded, then admitted, 'Dad and I often took a run up the river. Sometimes Mother came with us.' He helped her into the boat, then settled himself at the controls.

As they skimmed out towards the middle of the river she sent him a glance that was full of curiosity as she asked, 'Why are you taking me on these nostalgic trips? The lake, the beach, the tower are all places of sad memories for you.'

'Let's just say you're helping me lay ghosts. For years I've had no desire to do them alone, but now I'd like you to share them.'

The words caused her pulses to leap. What was he saying? She held her breath as she waited to hear more, but he remained silent. Then, greatly daring, she said softly, 'You need a mate.'

Again she held her breath, awaiting his reaction to this suggestion, but when he spoke his words came as an anti-climax.

'A mate? Well, maybe some day,' he murmured, turning the bow southwards towards the wider waters which rippled on their way to the Tasman Sea.

Her spirits took a downward dive, but she did her best to appear interested while he reminisced. And as the wind whipped her cheeks she listened to his recounting of tales his father had told about coastal shipping at the Port of Wanganui during the colony's early years, stories of ships being driven ashore to the black sands at Castlecliff, or grounded on the bar at the mouth of the river.

Dreamily she listened, knowing she would never tire of hearing the resonant timbre of his deep voice, and then a nervous gasp escaped her as the bow swung round in a wide half-circle and the boat headed north with foam spraying from the sides and stern.

As they left the city waters her eyes turned towards the tower on Durie Hill, and she recalled how her fear of the height had been brushed away by his kisses.

He followed the direction of her gaze then grinned as he said, 'You need have no fear of being dragged up there today.'

She pushed the memory of their embrace from her mind as riverside homes nestling behind trees caught her attention, and, making an effort to sound casual and to forget the tower, she said, 'There must be miles and miles of weeping willows.'

'Would you believe they are all descended from a willow growing beside Napoleon Bonaparte's grave on the island of St Helena? A cutting was brought home by an early missionary.' He told her how it had been nursed on board until it had reached home to take root and grow in the fertile Wanganui soil.

Moments later he pointed to port. 'The winery we visited it over there. You sampled sherry, remember?'

'And later became thoroughly uninhibited,' she admitted in a low voice, realising that this nostalgic trip was also becoming a momory trip for herself.

A short time later the hills on either side of the river closed in to narrow the valley. The strip of flat land bordering the water was thick with riverside growth, and his next words startled her.

'There they are, the clumps of pampas where we gathered the plumes. Can you see them?'

She stared at the tall feathery tops swaying in the breeze, a faint flush creeping into her cheeks as she recalled that

there, also, his arms had held her close to him. Did he
remember? His next words indicated that he did.

'I hope you have sufficient pampas, because I rather
hesitate to land for the purpose of gathering more.' His lips
twitched as he added, 'I might be given a poke in the eye.'

She stole a glance at him, but could find no reply.

'I'm referring to your workroom monologue,' he pursued.
'Isn't that what you threatened?'

'I was talking to myself. You weren't meant to hear.'

'But I did catch that muttered remark, and I must say it
gave me a shock. Until that moment I'd been under the
impression you'd enjoyed the moments of closeness we'd
shared. I even imagined you'd responded with more than a
little ardour, but now I can see that that's all it was, my
imagination.'

He paused, giving her the opportunity to make a reply,
but when she continued to remain silent he went on, 'Well,
I'd like to put your mind at rest. I want you to know you'll
have no more need to fear presumption on my part.'

A feeling of desperation gripped her. What was he
saying? Did he mean he had himself under such firm
control that there would be no further unguarded moments
when impulse caused him to snatch her to him? Or did he
mean that the desire to hold her close had evaporated?

Somehow she knew with certainty that those deliciously
unexpected moments that sent her up into the clouds were
at an end, and as she stared unseeingly at the green hills his
voice continued to depress her spirits.

'Actually, I'm surprised you agreed to come out with me
today, but perhaps you were unable to resist a run up the
river. Is that why you came?'

She nodded because her mind seemed to be unable to find
a reply to this accusation, and she was also aware of a
growing misery as the joy of this outing began to tumble
about her shoulders. Nor would her pride allow her to deny

that the river trip had been her main reason for coming out with him.

'You're very silent,' he remarked at last.

'I'm wondering why you're so intent upon ruining this day for me,' she said with an upsurge of irritation.

He shrugged. 'You can call it frustration.'

Her eyes widened as she turned to stare at him. '*Frustration*? What on earth do you mean? Really, I don't understand.'

'Then don't bother to try,' he advised crisply.

She waited, hoping for more explanation. Could it be possible he was torn between what he felt for her, and what he thought of her as a person? Did his kisses really mean more than he would allow himself to admit even to himself because he still held a lingering doubt about her desire for inheritance from her aunt?

His next words came as a warning. 'You'd better get ready to hold on tightly, because there are rapids ahead. Just give yourself up to the pleasures of skimming over them.'

'I'll do that,' she replied evenly, and from then on she made a determined effort to rise above her depression by concentrating on the grandeur of the scenery.

The river alternated between calm reaches and the swiftness of rapids where the foam flew and the boat almost left the water to leap across the shallow stony stretches. In many places the banks took the form of almost vertical mauve-grey cliffs which were patched with yellow and red clays. In some areas they were clothed with clinging fern and mosses, while above them the varied greens of the bush rose in precipitous slopes to more than a thousand feet.

In the calm reaches the scene became mirrored in the glassy water, taking on a dreamlike quality that seemed to transport them to a different world where there was only idyllic beauty.

Luke said, 'There are too many river places to visit in one afternoon. Apart from Maori villages there are tributaries to be navigated, waterfalls to be seen, and away up north there's the Bridge to Nowhere.'

'The Bridge to Nowhere?' she echoed.

'It's a large concrete structure built over fifty years ago to give access to farms, but I'm afraid those people have left the land which later became deserted, and all that remains is the bridge.'

The thought of the bridge caught her imagination. 'I know that bridge,' she declared impulsively.

His brows rose. 'You do? You've been on the river before?'

She shook her head. 'No—but *I know that bridge*. It's a dead end. I'm on it *right now*,' she added, her tongue running away with her as fanciful thoughts took charge.

He looked at her with concern. 'Are you feeling all right? You're looking rather pale. And I can only presume that you do know you're in a jet-boat, not on a bridge.'

She gave a small laugh. 'Please don't take any notice of me. I know I'm being stupid.' How could she explain that in coming from Palmerston North to Wanganui she had found the man she loved, the only man with whom she could spend the rest of her life? But as far as she could see that journey would end in nothing. She was on the bridge that would lead to nowhere. Hadn't he told her so? There would be no more kisses, he had said. Only he hadn't used the word 'kisses'. 'Presumption' was what he'd called it, the meaning being exactly the same.

He continued to observe her critically. 'You're looking very tired. I think we've come far enough. It's time we turned back.'

'Where does one go when one turns back?' she asked bleakly and with a faraway look in her eyes.

'One goes home, and right smartly,' he declared briskly.

'You may not realise it, but you're talking rather strangely. You don't sound like your usual self.'

Fleur took a quick peep at the lines of his straight nose and hard jaw, then looked down at the yellow jacket and leggings she was wearing. The sight of them jolted her into appreciating the fact that he had gone to the trouble of purchasing them for her to wear in this jet-boat, which had been specially hired to give her a trip up the river. He had been more than kind, while all she could do was become idiotic by allowing her emotions to cause stupid babblings.

She pulled herself together. 'I'm sorry if I've been sounding inane. It was really the thought of a bridge to nowhere that sent my imagination haywire.'

'Or did the rapids put you on edge? Many people are unnerved by them, so don't be afraid to admit it.'

'No, it wasn't the rapids. If you knew me better you'd realise there are times when I'm apt to chatter like a half-wit.'

He smiled. 'Let me assure you, I know you better than you think.'

His words did little to comfort her, and she could find nothing to say as he turned the bow of the boat and they set off down the river. The rapids were almost flown over, nor did he pause in the calm reaches where the jet splintered the silence as it sent sprays of foam towards the sides of the narrow gorges.

In one of these places they were made to realise they were not the only people on the river when noise other than their own echoed between the lofty walls. Hasty glances over their shoulders revealed a larger and swifter vessel, filled with happy, laughing teenagers, approaching from astern, and as it swept past its wash made their boat rock so violently it caused Fleur to shriek with terror and cling for safety, fearing she would be flung into the water.

The bow wave that crashed over their gunwale caused

them to become ankle-deep in water, and there was no escaping its drenching effect. The teenagers thought it hilarious, their merriment being evident as their craft headed for the next bend in the river.

Luke was not amused. He muttered angrily as he reduced speed, then gritted, 'There's a baler somewhere. See if you can get rid of that water, otherwise you'll have wet feet!'

'Wet feet—huh, you've got to be joking. They're swamped now.' She laughed shakily while reaching for the baler and immediately set to work, scooping up the water and throwing it over the side. At the same time she was grateful for action that would help disguise her fear from Luke's critical eyes.

As she worked her wet face stung from the coldness of the wind which was now blowing from the south, and she was more than thankful for the waterproof jacket she was wearing. Luke had bought it for her, she reminded herself. Yes, he was more than thoughtful.

He glanced at her feet, then offered advice. 'You'd be wise to remove those wet shoes and socks. They could give you a chill.'

'I've been thinking about it,' she said, frowning at her shoes and knowing this to be more than possible. She did not catch cold easily, but when she did it was usually caused by cold feet or a prolonged period in wet shoes. 'If I take them off my feet will become very cold, therefore I'm tossing up between freezing feet or wet feet. I think I'll leave them on and hope for the best.'

'We've a fair distance to go,' he warned. 'I've no wish to see you laid low with a cold.'

'At least not before Mrs Barker's baskets are finished,' she flashed at him in a jocular manner.

'To the devil with those dratted baskets,' he retorted tersely. 'I'm tired of hearing Jessica's constant satisfied yacker about such a good order being so well attended to.'

She took a deep breath. 'Are you saying you regret that I stayed to complete it for her?'

'Of course not. I mean I consider it was an imposition for her to have expected you to do it.' He paused before asking, 'When will the job be finished?'

'If I really set my mind to it, it could be done by Wednesday. And then I'll be on my way.'

She waited, hoping for even the slightest sound of regret, but no sign of it came. Instead he sent the jet-boat speeding down the river, yet despite his haste and the clothing she wore, her teeth were chattering by the time they reached the boat landing.

No time was wasted in getting her into the car where her wet shoes and socks were whipped from her feet. The Volvo's heater was switched on, and he made an effort to warm her feet by massaging them with his hands.

His action caused her pulses to race. She yearned to reach with her own hands to touch his bent head and run her fingers through his dark hair, but she resisted the impulse. Instead she just spoke quietly. 'Thank you, Luke. You certainly know how to take care of—of a person. Please believe I'll never forget this day.'

CHAPTER TEN

IT WAS almost dark when they reached home. Luke stopped the Volvo near the steps leading up to the back veranda, then said to Fleur, 'If I let you out here you'll have no need to walk across the gravel with bare feet. The stones are hard.'

'Thank you,' she said, appreciating his thoughtfulness.

She got out and went up the steps while he garaged the car, but when she carried her wet shoes and socks into the kitchen she was greeted by a baleful glare from Carla.

'Oh, so you're home *at last*.' The blonde then eyed her bare feet with a hint of surprise, her lip curling slightly as she added, 'Don't tell me you've been paddling.'

Fleur forced a smile, refusing to take offence at the sarcastic tone. 'That's right but only in the bottom of the boat.'

'You mean it leaked?'

'Not exactly. I'll explain later, but first I'd prefer to change into other clothes.'

Carla stared at the yellow parka and leggings. 'You'd better give those things to me. I'll hang them in the laundry. Hurry up, get them off.'

'You mean—this jacket?'

'Of course. What else? Surely you didn't imagine they'd been given to you? They were only *lent* to be worn on the river.'

Fleur was startled. 'I see. Yes, of course I understand.' But she hadn't understood, and now wondered how she could have been naïve enough to believe they had

170

been gifts.

Carla's voice became cold with barely suppressed anger. 'It was utterly ridiculous for Luke to have gone to that expense. Come on, give them to me at once,' she snapped impatiently.

Fleur sent her a cool stare. 'Certainly not. Luke lent them to me, therefore I'll return them to him.' And with that decision she left the kitchen to hasten upstairs where a hot shower removed the chill which, despite the car's heater, had gripped her body during the drive home.

The soothing waters also did much to wash away the irritation of Carla's words, and Fleur called herself an idiot for having jumped to the conclusion that the jacket and leggings had been a gift. Naturally he had bought them only for her to wear when on the river, and thank heavens Carla had pointed this out before she'd taken them home. The thought that she might have done so gave her a feeling of horror. It would be like stealing them.

When she went downstairs she discovered Luke talking with Carla in the front hall. The blonde was smiling up into his face and Fleur hesitated to intrude into their conversation, but as she began to walk towards the living-room Luke eyed the garments she carried over her arm.

'Where are you going with that yellow-wear?' he asked. 'Not back to the river, I hope.'

She glanced at Carla then said, 'I'm returning them to you. Thank you for the loan of them.'

His expression changed. 'The loan? Are you saying you have no wish to accept them as a gift?'

'Carla told me—I mean, I was given to understand you were lending them to me.'

Carla flushed as she cut in to speak to Luke. 'Well, naturally I presumed you were only lending them to her. She's not likely to find use for them in Palmerston North.'

His eyes held a veiled expression. 'Aren't you forgetting

that Palmerston North is on the Manawatu River? Fleur's friend, Mr Quinn, might take her boating on it. I can just see them, rowing up the river.'

'That's most unlikely,' Fleur retorted, irritated.

Luke turned to her. 'Then please accept them gracefully. Take them to your room because they're yours to keep.'

'Oh, thank you, Luke,' she breathed, her heart lifting as she realised the garments were indeed a gift. But as she turned to go upstairs she caught a glimpse of bitter hatred flashing from Carla's hazel eyes.

The rest of the evening passed quietly and with most of the dinner conversation revolving round the various houses Jessica had viewed during the last few days. There was still one she was particularly interested in and she would be grateful for Luke's opinion of it.

Luke, who had listened to her chatter without comment, reminded her there was no need for them to leave Rivermoon, but Jessica swept the suggestion aside, and again became adamant about having her own home. Luke then pushed his chair back from the table, saying he must attend to farm accounts.

As Fleur watched him go through the door she felt that a vital force had left the room. She began to feel weary, and she also became conscious of the dislike lurking behind some of Carla's veiled glances, therefore she excused herself and went to bed early.

But as she lay between the sheets her thoughts became depressed. Carla looked upon her as an enemy, she realised, although this was something she had known during her entire period at Rivermoon. However, there was little she could do about it, and as she stared into the darkness Carla's face was replaced by a vision of Luke's dark grey eyes and sensuous mouth.

During the day he'd made no attempt to kiss her, she recalled sadly. There had been no reaching to draw her closer to him, although there had been plenty of opportunity, with only the birds to observe an embrace.

A poke in the eye was what he had feared, or so he had said, which was utter nonsense because he knew she had always responded to his kisses. It all added up to the sad fact that he no longer wished to kiss her, or to hold her in his arms. The fear of a poke in the eye was merely an excuse. A polite backing away.

Tears rolled down her face, soaking into the pillow as she recalled that first day when he had walked into the Fleurette. Just a small amount of assistance for Jessica, he had requested. And while she had not been averse to the thought of seeing him again, she had also hoped there would be the chance of a reconciliation between her mother and her aunt.

For Pete's sake, she had now been here for almost a month. And what had been the result? She herself had fallen in love with Luke, while reconciliation between the two sisters was as distant as ever. They would come together only when a crisis of some sort made it necessary, and until then it would remain a hopeless case.

As for her own situation, that also appeared to be a hopeless case, and she could see that the longer she stayed at Rivermoon the more miserable she would become.

When Fleur woke next morning her head felt heavy but she ignored the discomfort and went to breakfast earlier than usual. The men were still at the table and Luke sent her a critical glance as he said, 'You're looking rather pale. Are you feeling all right?'

'I'm fine,' she lied. 'Mrs Barker is coming today, so I'm making an early start.'

Bob spoke in a voice that was like a low growl. 'Today's the day when Elaine Barker will learn the truth. I've warned Jessica that if she doesn't come clean about who is making these baskets I'll tell the woman myself. It's downright deception, and I don't like it.'

Luke said, 'You can stop worrying about it, Bob. Elaine Barker is well aware that Fleur is making them.'

'She is?' Fleur's eyes widened with surprise. 'How does she know? Are you saying that Aunt Jess told her?'

Luke uttered a short laugh. 'No, I'm saying that I told her. As Bob says, it was deceitful of Jess to allow her to think that she was making them, so I told her exactly whose hands were doing the work. Besides, it annoyed me to know that this lie was being perpetrated from Rivermoon.'

His last statement did not surprise Fleur, nor did she find difficulty in understanding his feelings. He was a man of integrity, and he expected honesty from the people living in his home. 'When did you tell her?' she asked.

'When you completed the first lot of baskets,' he admitted. 'That's why she came back so smartly with such a large order. She was snatching at the opportunity to build up a backlog of stock while you were available to do so.'

'That woman's nobody's fool,' Bob observed with conviction. 'I must say, I'm relieved that she knows the truth.'

Fleur also felt relieved, and when Mrs Barker arrived to collect the next batch of completed baskets she found herself feeling more at ease with Jessica's client. However, she found difficulty in hiding her mirth when Jessica made an admission.

'Perhaps I should explain that Fleur has been helping me,' she said to Elaine Barker. 'You see, it's my hands . . .'

Elaine flicked an amused glance towards Fleur, but her voice held sympathy as she said, 'I understand. It must be terribly difficult for you.'

'Not only difficult, but painful,' Jessica sighed. 'I'm afraid I'll be forced to give up the work, especially as I'll be moving into a new house with very little garden attached to it.' She went on to enthuse about her plans for having her own home.

Fleur helped to carry the baskets out to Elaine Barker's station wagon, and as the vehicle disappeared down the drive she realised that only a few more were needed to complete the order. The job was almost finished.

But when she returned to the workroom she found herself moving slowly, not only because she had no wish to finish the job which would herald her departure, but also because her head still felt heavy. And by evening it was accompanied by a sore throat.

She went to bed early, hoping that these annoyances would disappear during the night, but next morning they were still there, and if anything slightly worse. However, she brushed them aside, telling herself they would soon pass, and went to the workroom where the constant use of tissues became necessary.

Jessica dosed her with aspirin. She did all she could to assist with the few remaining baskets, and by Tuesday evening there were only three left to be done. But by that time Fleur had developed a slight cough.

Again she went to bed early, but before going upstairs she prepared a mixture of lemon and honey to be taken with more aspirin.

Carla stood beside her at the bench, a faint sneer twisting her lips. 'You're sure taking good care of yourself. Anyone would imagine you considered yourself to be ill,' she declared scathingly.

'I know it's only a cold, but I've no wish for it to become worse,' Fleur defended.

'It's hardly a cold. A mere sniffle is all I'd call it.'

'But then *you* are not troubled by it.'

'You're making a ton of fuss over nothing. You're putting on a show of coughing and sneezing for Luke's benefit,' accused Carla.

'Why should I do that?'

'Because you're looking for sympathy, of course. And don't leave that bench in a mess. See that you wipe it clean.'

'I'll do that,' Fleur promised.

When she reached her bedroom she could hear the cold south-westerly wind howling about the house. It sent rain beating against the balcony door, and as she drew the curtains the trickles running down the glass reminded her of tears.

They gave her the feeling of being very much in tune with the weather—miserable, depressed. But not cold like the outside atmosphere, because the bed had been heated to a state of luxury by the electric blanket. Yet despite its delicious warmth she continued to cough until she feared she must be disturbing the rest of the household.

It was midnight when the door opened and Luke walked into the room. The woollen tartan dressing-gown he wore over his pyjamas was blue and green with a yellow stripe, and as she looked at him through watery eyes she saw that he carried a small packet in his hand.

'I'm sorry if I've been keeping you awake,' she said huskily.

'No, I was reading.' He stared at her in silence for several moments then said, 'You've certainly caught a rotten cold. Those wet feet on Sunday, I suppose.'

She nodded, unable to speak as she reached towards the box of tissues.

He regarded her critically. 'You're lying too low. Your head needs to be raised, and I've brought you cough squares.'

'What are they?'

He sat on the side of the bed while he opened the packet, then removed a lozenge from its foil wrapping and popped it into her mouth. 'Just suck it,' he advised.

'Thank you, you're always so good,' she muttered.

His voice became stern. 'Tomorrow you'll stay in bed.'

She shook her head then croaked, 'Only three more baskets to do.'

'They can wait.'

'I'll do them, then come back to bed.'

'You're as stubborn as your aunt and your mother.'

Again she shook her head, although it hurt her to do so. 'Not really. It's just that Aunt promised Mrs Barker she could have them on Wednesday afternoon, so I'll do my best to get them done.'

Luke frowned. 'She must have forgotten she's going out tomorrow afternoon. She has arranged for me to accompany Bob and herself for a further examination of this house she's so keen to buy.'

'Oh, well, I can attend to Mrs Barker.'

'It's a pity you can't come with us, but you're definitely not stepping outside the door. In any case it'll be a lousy day. The weather report has promised us more of the same.'

She sent him a wan smile. 'I promise—not a step outside the door will I take.'

'Good. Now where's your other pillow? There are two on every bed in this house.'

'It's on the top wardrobe shelf.'

He found the extra pillow, then bent over her to place it in position beneath her head. As he did so his dressing-gown fell open to reveal a bare chest lightly covered with crisp dark hairs. Her raised cheek almost brushed them, and she knew an almost overwhelming desire to lay her lips against his throat. Then her heart leapt as his arms went about her shoulders to clasp her against him.

'Just get rid of this blasted cold,' he murmured above her head. 'We have to talk.'

'Talk?' Her heart gave another leap as she felt his lips press her forehead.

But suddenly the spell was broken as Carla's voice spoke

from behind them. 'What's going on. Is she dying?'

Luke glanced over his shoulder. 'Not yet. She's having her head raised and I've given her cough suppressants.' Then to Fleur he added, 'You may take two every three hours.'

'Thank you.' She smiled at him gratefully, conscious that her spirits had lifted. Luke had held her close to him.

Carla's eyes glittered with suspicion as they moved from one to the other. 'I heard voices and wondered if she was OK.'

'She will be now.' Luke's voice was nonchalant as he ushered Carla out of the room and closed the door.

The next day saw little improvement in Fleur's condition, and while she longed to remain in bed it was sheer determination that sent her to the workroom, where she toiled until she was able to stand back and view the last three baskets with a sense of satisfaction. However, when she called for Jessica's approval of the finished work her aunt showed little interest, because her mind seemed to be fully occupied with her housing project.

'I'm sorry you're not well enough to come with us to see the place,' she said to Fleur. 'I've invited Carla also, but she said she felt she should remain at home to take care of you.'

Fleur was indignant. 'Take care of *me*? That's ridiculous. Besides, I don't want her to take care of me.'

'Well, you must admit it's rather sweet of her,' said Jessica. 'However, you'll both see the place quite soon.'

'Then your mind is made up about it?'

'Yes, it's exactly what I want, but Bob feels he'd like Luke's approval of it.' She sent an impatient glance towards her watch. 'We're due to meet the agent at two o'clock, so if Elaine Barker hasn't come by that time you'll have to give her this last batch.'

'I'll attend to it, Aunt.'

'And as soon as the baskets have gone, you must go

straight to bed.'

'I'll do that,' Fleur promised, feeling she could not get there quickly enough.

However, Elaine Barker had not arrived by the time they left, and as Fleur watched the Volvo splash through puddles on the drive the chilly air made her shiver. She sent glances towards the dripping trees and knew that the dark clouds overhead meant more rain.

She then set herself the task of tidying the workroom which was now in a state of disorder with scraps of dried flowers, cut stems and unrolled ribbons lying about the bench and floor. And by the time she had finished sweeping, her heavy cold was making her feel weary.

It was after three-thirty before Elaine Barker rang the front doorbell. The baskets were loaded into her vehicle, and Fleur knew a sense of relief as she watched it depart. She then mixed herself a dose of honey and lemon and carried it upstairs.

She met Carla on the landing but it was not until later that she realised the blonde had been waiting for her.

Carla eyed the glass of lemon and honey. 'You're going back to bed?'

'Yes.' Fleur entered her room.

Carla followed, an affable smile on her face. 'Let me help you to get undressed.'

Fleur laughed as she placed the lemon and honey on the bedside table. 'Don't be silly, I can undress myself.'

Carla stood still, staring at something that had caught her attention through the glass door. 'What's that object out on the balcony? Does it belong to you?'

Fleur moved nearer the door, then peered at the long woollen blue and green article lying in a twisted heap on the balcony floor. 'I believe it's the girdle from Luke's dressing-gown. How on earth could it get out there?' she asked with surprise.

She opened the door then stepped out quickly to snatch up the wet girdle, but before she could whip back into the room the door had been slammed shut. She grabbed the handle, turning it frantically, but found the key had been turned, and she was then shocked to see Carla grinning maliciously through the glass.

'That'll teach you to entice Luke into your room,' the blonde shouted at her. 'I know he was kissing you.'

'Carla, let me in, I'm getting wet,' Fleur cried.

'Get yourself in,' Carla yelled at her. 'You can go down the fire escape, it never gets any use, so you can give it some.'

Fleur rushed to Luke's bedroom door which also opened on to the balcony, but of course it was locked, and it was then she realised that Carla had carefully planned this situation.

She then peered over the balustrade at a ladder attached to a nearby wall. From where she stood she could see its rungs went only a certain distance, and then she would have to jump to the ground. To escape by it meant climbing over and reaching for it, but a glance downwards was enough to bring a surge of her fear of heights and to send her reeling back to hammer at the door.

'*Carla, Carla*, I can't do it. Let me in, *please!*'

But there was no reply. Carla had left the room.

She'll come back, Fleur assured herself. She *must* come back and let me in. But although she waited and waited, shivering in the cold while the pouring rain soaked through to her skin, there was no sign of Carla's return, and at last a spasm of coughing warned that she must make an attempt on the fire escape.

A leg over the balustrade with one hand gripping the rail enabled her to reach for the ladder rung, and, not daring to look down, she remained in that position while taking several deep breaths in an attempt to control her violent shaking. But eventually she became calm enough to draw her other leg across, then slowly made her way down the ladder until she knew she was at the end of its short length.

After that she wasn't sure whether she had jumped, or whether she had lost her grip and fallen, but she found herself lying sprawled in the wet mud of the garden.

The feel of it sent her scrambling to her feet, and she ran round the house from one door to another, only to find them locked, while the downstairs windows were also securely fastened. Her teeth were chattering from the cold, and it was while she was again banging desperately at the back door that the Volvo swung into the yard.

Luke slammed on the brakes then leapt from the car to stride to her. 'What the devil are you doing out here?' he demanded furiously. 'Good grief, you're soaking wet.'

She leaned against him, shaking and weeping piteously, her words almost incoherent between sobs and a further onset of coughing as she stammered, 'C-Carla—C-Carla—l-locked me—out——'

He hammered on the door, which was opened by a white-faced Carla. 'What the hell's going on?' he roared.

'It—it was only a joke,' she tried to assure him, her face now betraying fright.

'How long has she been out in this weather?' he snapped. 'And what the devil is she doing with my dressing-gown girdle tied round her waist?'

Carla began to shed tears. 'It was nothing. I didn't mean any real harm to come to her.'

'I'll talk to you later. I'll get to the bottom of this.'

Fleur became vaguely aware that Jessica and Bob had joined them and that Luke was issuing orders. To Bob he said, 'Ring the doctor. Explain her condition and suggest he brings antibiotics with him. Warn him he could find pleurisy, pneumonia or at least a case of flu.' To Jessica he said, 'Come with me and get her into bed.' He then lifted

Fleur into his arms and carried her up the stairs.

A short time later the warmth of the electric blanket began to relax her nervous tension. She did not believe the doctor would consider she was suffering from either pleurisy or pneumonia, but because her body ached all over, and her head felt ready to split open while her throat burned with a stinging pain, she suspected she now had a severe dose of the flu.

The doctor arrived in a surprisingly short time, perhaps because he happened to be one of Bob's friends. She sat up while his stethoscope moved over her back and chest, but her mind was in such a dazed state his diagnosis hardly registered with her. However, she swallowed his pills and within a short time she had fallen asleep.

She slept for at least four hours before waking to lie in a dreamy state with closed eyes, and being vaguely conscious of hearing voices. Her aunt's voice was easily recognised, but the other—surely it couldn't be *Mother*? Or was she dreaming?

She opened her eyes slightly to observe her mother and aunt sitting on either side of the bed, their faces dimmed by the shaded bedside light. They were speaking in low tones, each telling the other of incidents that had occurred during the last ten years. Listening, it seemed to Fleur that the barrier between them had been finally removed, or at least lowered to a surprising extent.

At last she spoke. 'Mother?'

Joyce turned to her quickly. 'Darling, you're awake. How do you feel?'

'Ghastly. My neck feels swollen. When did you come?'

Jessica cut in briskly. 'I rang your mother and she came at once. Now then, it's time for your next pill. You're to have one every four hours according to the doctor's orders.'

At that moment Luke came into the room. 'I believe it's pill time,' he said, echoing Jessica's words.

'I was just about to administer it,' she told him.

'I'll attend to it,' he told her. 'You two must have so much to discuss, and you're probably tired of talking in whispers. Why not continue beside the living-room fire?'

They glanced at each other, then almost scuttled from the room as though dismissed by the headmaster.

Luke moved to the bedside, then handed her a tablet. He poured water into a glass, and as she raised herself from the pillow his arm went about her shoulders for support. Even in her poor state his touch sent her pulses pounding.

She swallowed the pill and he lowered her gently to the pillow. 'I'm sorry to be such an idiot,' she muttered huskily.

He replaced the glass on the bedside table then sat in the chair recently vacated by her mother. Pulling it closer to the bed he leaned forward to look at her with concern in his eyes then asked, 'Is your throat too painful to talk?'

'No.' It wasn't the truth, but if Luke wished to talk she would make the effort.

He said, 'I'd be interested to learn how the girdle of my dressing-gown came to be round your waist.'

She smiled faintly. 'Didn't you ask Carla?'

'Yes. She declared she knew nothing about it.'

'Where did you last leave your girdle?'

'It never leaves my dressing-gown. It's always left twisted through the loops so that I don't lose it. That's why I can't understand how you came to have it. Nothing will make me believe you took it from my room.' His eyes became penetrating as he awaited her reply.

'Is that what Carla said, that I took it from your room?'

'Well, she hinted that such was highly probable.'

'It was out in the rain, lying on the balcony, and if anyone took it from your room it was Carla herself. When I was going back to bed she came into the room and pointed it out to me. I dashed out quickly to grab it, but before I could get in again she'd locked the door.' The enormity of Carla's action made her add, 'She must hate me very much.'

'And then?' he demanded quietly.

'She yelled at me to use the fire escape.'

'She remembered your fear of heights,' he pointed out grimly. 'Well, naturally she'll have to leave. There's not room in this house for both of us.'

'I don't understand. Aunt needs her, and I won't be here.'

He looked at her in silence for several long moments before he said, 'You'll recall that last night I said we had to talk?'

She nodded without speaking, wondering what he had in mind.

'It's about us. You're probably well aware that I love you very much.' The words came as a simple statement.

Her mouth opened but no sound came.

He went on, 'The thought of life in this house without you is intolerable. I love you so dearly, I can't let you go.'

She felt so overwhelmed her eyes filled with tears but still she remained silent, plagued by the feeling that this was a dream.

He said, 'You have nothing to say. In that case I'll quite understand that the idea of marrying me is abhorrent.'

His last words brought a cry of protest from her. '*Abhorrent*? No—no, Luke—*I love you.*' She sat up abruptly, reaching her hands towards him.

In a flash his arms were about her, holding her tightly against his breast. 'My darling, my darling——' he murmured above her head. 'You'll marry me?'

She nodded, clinging to him, her heart pounding with joy.

'Soon, my dearest. There's to be no long engagement, I hope. Rivermoon is waiting for its new mistress.'

She laughed happily, then promised, 'We'll be married just as soon as it can be arranged, although Mother and

Aunt will expect us to be engaged for what they consider to be a suitable period.'

'Then let's hope there'll be no clash between their idea of a suitable period and our own wishes. There's to be no further disagreement in this family, especially as they appear to be making a new beginning. With luck it will blossom into friendship.'

She spoke seriously. 'Be assured our engagement will be for only as long as it takes to make arrangements. Mother will have to replace me at the Fleurette.'

'And I'll find a replacement for Carla. My bride is not to become a slave to the Rivermoon homestead. My mother always had help in the house, usually a capable, middle-aged woman.' He paused to look at her thoughtfully. 'Do my reminiscences bore you?'

'No, of course not,' she responded earnestly, clasping his hand. 'They help me to see into your past and to know you better.'

He looked down at her fingers, then raised them to his lips. 'There's a small matter of an engagement ring. Would it interest you to see the one my mother wore?'

'Yes, of course.'

He left the room and Fleur heard him go to his bedroom. Would he come back, or was this only a dream? Had the doctor's drugs affected her brain? At least they were making her head and throat feel better. But it was not a dream because moments later Luke returned with two small boxes. Two boxes? Was she seeing double? No, of course not, because there was only one Luke.

He opened one to reveal a diamond solitaire ring, the size and brilliance of the stone almost taking her breath away. 'It's—*gorgeous*,' she exclaimed in a husky voice.

'You may wear it if you wish, unless you prefer that we choose a different type of ring together. It's your choice.'

'I couldn't wish for a more beautiful ring,' she said,

feeling overawed by the quality of the diamond.

'I was hoping you'd accept it,' he said. 'I must admit I'll be more than happy to see it flashing under the living-room lights again, especially when being worn by my wife.' He slipped it on her finger, then held her close to him while murmuring endearments.

Again Fleur felt herself to be in a dream as she made an effort to adjust her mind to the fact that she was now engaged to Luke, but at last curiosity forced her to ask, 'Didn't I see you with two boxes? What's in the other?'

'Your wedding ring,' he told her nonchalantly. 'Would you care to see it?'

'Yes, yes, please show it to me,' she pleaded, making no attempt to hide her excitement. But when he flicked the lid open she could only stare at the glistening band. 'That's a wedding ring—with diamonds all the way round?'

'Father had it specially made. It's taken me a long time to find the right finger to wear it. And now, my darling, it's time you went to sleep.

She stared at him bright-eyed. 'Sleep? You've got to be joking.'

Neverthless she did sleep. The antibiotics played their part and within a few days she was well enough to leave her bed.

Before leaving for Palmerston North she was taken to see Jessica's new house, and she also met the kindly woman Luke had engaged as a housekeeper. Fleur liked her at once, recognising in her a person who would guide her faltering steps as a newly-wed.

And then the day came when she walked up the long aisle of the old brick church on her father's arm. Radiant in her bridal gown and veil, she knew vaguely that her mother had surpassed herself with the church flowers, but she had eyes only for Luke, who waited for her near the altar.

He turned to watch her coming towards him, and as she

drew near he took several steps to meet her, his hand outstretched to clasp her own. 'My precious darling,' was all he had time to say.

HARLEQUIN
Romance

Coming Next Month

#3025 ARAFURA PIRATE Victoria Gordon
Jinx had been warned about Race Morgan, skipper of the boat taking her
scientific research team to Australia's northern coast. But she's confident she
can handle it, as long as he keeps their relationship professional.

#3026 GAME PLAN Rosemary Hammond
Jake Donovan, so everyone says, has an infallible plan that makes the women
fall at his feet. However, when it doesn't work with reserved Claire Talbot, he
finds to his surprise that he can't forget her. . . .

#3027 SPELL OF THE MOUNTAINS Rosalie Henaghan
Sophie is determined to make a success of her motel—and has no intention of
selling out to the powerful, dynamic hotelier Jon Roberts. Her refusal only
sparks his determination, for Jon isn't used to women who say no!

#3028 JINXED Day Leclaire
Kit soon discovers that playing with toys all day can be a dangerous
occupation, especially when working for a man like Stephen "The Iceman"
St. Clair. The normally cold and stern owner of The Toy Company behaves
more like a volcano whenever Kit is around.

#3029 CONFLICT Margaret Mayo
Blythe's first priority after her father's death is to make the family business
pay—and especially to prevent it from falling into Coburn Daggart's hands.
Years ago, Coburn hurt her badly, and Blythe makes up her mind to pay
him back.

#3030 FOOLISH DECEIVER Sandra K. Rhoades
Allie has learned the hard way that men don't like intelligent women. So, on
vacation at an old girlfriend's, she conceals her genius IQ. Her scheme
backfires when Linc Summerville believes she is a dumb blonde and treats her
like a fool!

Available in January wherever paperback books are sold, or through
Harlequin Reader Service:

In the U.S.
901 Fuhrmann Blvd.
P.O. Box 1397
Buffalo, N.Y. 14240-1397

In Canada
P.O. Box 603
Fort Erie, Ontario
L2A 5X3

CHRISTMAS IS FOR KIDS

Spend this holiday season with nine very special children. Children whose wishes come true at the magical time of Christmas.

Read American Romance's CHRISTMAS IS FOR KIDS— heartwarming holiday stories in which children bring together four couples who fall in love. Meet:

Frank, Dorcas, Kathy, Candy and Nicky—They become friends at St. Christopher's orphanage, but they really want to be adopted and become part of a real family, in #321 *A Carol Christmas* by Muriel Jensen.

Patty—She's a ten-year-old certified genius, but she wants what every little girl wishes for: a daddy of her own, in #322 *Mrs. Scrooge* by Barbara Bretton.

Amy and Flash—Their mom is about to deliver their newest sibling any day, but Christmas just isn't the same now—not without their dad. More than anything they want their family reunited for Christmas, in #323 *Dear Santa* by Margaret St. George.

Spencer—Living with his dad and grandpa in an all-male household has its advantages, but Spence wants Santa to bring him a mommy to love, in #324 *The Best Gift of All* by Andrea Davidson.

These children will win your hearts as they entice—and matchmake—the adults into a true romance. This holiday, invite them—and the four couples they bring together—into your home.

Look for all four CHRISTMAS IS FOR KIDS books available now from Harlequin American Romance. And happy holidays!

XMAS-KIDS-1R

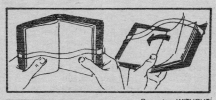

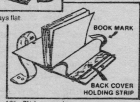

INDULGE A LITTLE SWEEPSTAKES

OFFICIAL RULES

SWEEPSTAKES RULES AND REGULATIONS. NO PURCHASE NECESSARY.

1. NO PURCHASE NECESSARY. To enter complete the official entry form and return with the invoice in the envelope provided. Or you may enter by printing your name, complete address and your daytime phone number on a 3 x 5 piece of paper. Include with your entry the hand printed words "Indulge A Little Sweepstakes." Mail your entry to: Indulge A Little Sweepstakes, P.O. Box 1397, Buffalo, NY 14269-1397. No mechanically reproduced entries accepted. Not responsible for late, lost, misdirected mail, or printing errors.

2. Three winners, one per month (Sept. 30, 1989, October 31, 1989 and November 30, 1989), will be selected in random drawings. All entries received prior to the drawing date will be eligible for that month's prize. This sweepstakes is under the supervision of MARDEN-KANE, INC. an independent judging organization whose decisions are final and binding. Winners will be notified by telephone and may be required to execute an affidavit of eligibility and release which must be returned within 14 days, or an alternate winner will be selected.

3. Prizes: 1st Grand Prize (1) a trip for two to Disneyworld in Orlando, Florida. Trip includes round trip air transportation, hotel accommodations for seven days and six nights, plus up to $700 expense money (ARV $3,500). 2nd Grand Prize (1) a seven-night Chandris Caribbean Cruise for two includes transportation from nearest major airport, accommodations, meals plus up to $1,000 in expense money (ARV $4,300). 3rd Grand Prize (1) a ten day Hawaiian holiday for two includes round trip air transportation for two, hotel accommodations, sightseeing, plus up to $1,200 in spending money (ARV $7,700). All trips subject to availability and must be taken as outlined on the entry form.

4. Sweepstakes open to residents of the U.S. and Canada 18 years or older except employees and the families of Torstar Corp., its affiliates, subsidiaries and Marden-Kane, Inc. and all other agencies and persons connected with conducting this sweepstakes. All Federal, State and local laws and regulations apply. Void wherever prohibited or restricted by law. Taxes, if any are the sole responsibility of the prize winners. Canadian winners will be required to answer a skill testing question. Winners consent to the use of their name, photograph and/or likeness for publicity purposes without additional compensation.

5. For a list of prize winners, send a stamped, self-addressed envelope to Indulge A Little Sweepstakes Winners, P.O. Box 701, Sayreville, NJ 08871.

© 1989 HARLEQUIN ENTERPRISES LTD.

DL-SWPS

INDULGE A LITTLE SWEEPSTAKES

OFFICIAL RULES

SWEEPSTAKES RULES AND REGULATIONS. NO PURCHASE NECESSARY.

1. NO PURCHASE NECESSARY. To enter complete the official entry form and return with the invoice in the envelope provided. Or you may enter by printing your name, complete address and your daytime phone number on a 3 x 5 piece of paper. Include with your entry the hand printed words "Indulge A Little Sweepstakes." Mail your entry to: Indulge A Little Sweepstakes, P.O. Box 1397 Buffalo, NY 14269-1397. No mechanically reproduced entries accepted. Not responsible for late, lost, misdirected mail, or printing errors.

2. Three winners, one per month (Sept. 30, 1989, October 31, 1989 and November 30, 1989), will be selected in random drawings. All entries received prior to the drawing date will be eligible for that month's prize. This sweepstakes is under the supervision of MARDEN-KANE, INC. an independent judging organization whose decisions are final and binding. Winners will be notified by telephone and may be required to execute an affidavit of eligibility and release which must be returned within 14 days, or an alternate winner will be selected.

3. Prizes: 1st Grand Prize (1) a trip for two to Disneyworld in Orlando, Florida. Trip includes round trip air transportation, hotel accommodations for seven days and six nights, plus up to $700 expense money (ARV $3,500). 2nd Grand Prize (1) a seven-night Chandris Caribbean Cruise for two includes transportation from nearest major airport, accommodations, meals plus up to $1,000 in expense money (ARV $4,300). 3rd Grand Prize (1) a ten-day Hawaiian holiday for two includes round trip air transportation for two, hotel accommodations, sightseeing, plus up to $1,200 in spending money (ARV $7,700). All trips subject to availability and must be taken as outlined on the entry form.

4. Sweepstakes open to residents of the U.S. and Canada 18 years or older except employees and the families of Torstar Corp., its affiliates, subsidiaries and Marden-Kane, Inc. and all other agencies and persons connected with conducting this sweepstakes. All Federal, State and local laws and regulations apply. Void wherever prohibited or restricted by law. Taxes, if any are the sole responsibility of the prize winners. Canadian winners will be required to answer a skill testing question. Winners consent to the use of their name, photograph and/or likeness for publicity purposes without additional compensation.

5. For a list of prize winners, send a stamped, self-addressed envelope to Indulge A Little Sweepstakes Winners, P.O. Box 701, Sayreville, NJ 08871.

© 1989 HARLEQUIN ENTERPRISES LTD.

DL-SWPS

INDULGE A LITTLE—WIN A LOT!

Summer of '89 Subscribers-Only Sweepstakes

OFFICIAL ENTRY FORM

This entry must be received by: Nov. 30, 1989
This month's winner will be notified by: Dec. 7, 1989
Trip must be taken between: Jan. 7, 1990–Jan. 7, 1991

YES, I want to win the 3-Island Hawaiian vacation for two! I understand the prize includes round-trip airfare, first-class hotels, and a daily allowance as revealed on the "Wallet" scratch-off card.

Name_____

Address_____

City_____ State/Prov._____ Zip/Postal Code_____

Daytime phone number_____
                                    Area code

Return entries with invoice in envelope provided. Each book in this shipment has two entry coupons — and the more coupons you enter, the better your chances of winning!

© 1989 HARLEQUIN ENTERPRISES LTD.

DINDL-3

INDULGE A LITTLE—WIN A LOT!

Summer of '89 Subscribers-Only Sweepstakes

OFFICIAL ENTRY FORM

This entry must be received by: Nov. 30, 1989
This month's winner will be notified by: Dec. 7, 1989
Trip must be taken between: Jan. 7, 1990–Jan. 7, 1991

YES, I want to win the 3-Island Hawaiian vacation for two! I understand the prize includes round-trip airfare, first-class hotels, and a daily allowance as revealed on the "Wallet" scratch-off card.

Name_____

Address_____

City_____ State/Prov._____ Zip/Postal Code_____

Daytime phone number_____
                                    Area code

Return entries with invoice in envelope provided. Each book in this shipment has two entry coupons — and the more coupons you enter, the better your chances of winning!

© 1989 HARLEQUIN ENTERPRISES LTD.

DINDL-3